LEADER OF THE RESISTANCE

The Fitzroy Edition of

JULES VERNE

Edited by I. O. Evans

LEADER
OF THE RESISTANCE

by

JULES VERNE

Part I

of

FAMILY WITHOUT A NAME

Edited by

I. O. EVANS

F.R.G.S.

LONDON
ARCO PUBLICATIONS
1963

First published 1963 by Arco Publications

© Arco Publications 1963

Printed in Northern Ireland by
W. & G. Baird Ltd., Union Street, Belfast 1

CONTENTS

CONTENTS

INTRODUCTION

WE LEARNED in school that Canada was won for what was once called the British Empire when Wolfe defeated Montcalm on the heights of Abraham above Quebec, both these heroes falling gloriously in battle. Then, probably, most of us in Britain—if we thought about it at all—took it for granted that the people of Quebec Province, overjoyed at being ' rescued ' from French rule, at once settled down as loyal British subjects to live happily ever after.

Needless to say, this naïve view is very far from the truth: the people of Quebec would have been only too happy to remain under the French Crown. They were themselves French, and they regarded the British conquest as a cruel tyranny and usurpation; nor are they entirely reconciled to it to-day. There is indeed a ' Separatist ' Movement astir in Quebec; hence this little-known Verne story is of immediate topical interest.

As might be expected, the movement includes many diverse elements, and has its extremist fringe who seek Quebec's complete independence not only from the British Commonwealth but from the rest of Canada. With some it even rankles that the Canadian Flag should include the British emblem, which they regard as symbolising an alien conquest.

The more moderate Separatists, however, treat such

symbolic grievances as a mere fogging of the issue, and regard the complete independence of Quebec as undesirable, if not impossible. It would lead, they suspect, to the rest of Canada's joining the United States, and this would mean that Quebec itself, as a mere French-speaking enclave in an American-speaking continent, could no longer exist separately; it too would be forced willy-nilly to merge into the augmented U.S.A., with a complete loss of its present individuality. Their own aim is much more practical. It may be summed up as greater recognition and status throughout Canada for the French Canadians, many of whom feel that they are not regarded seriously enough either by their compatriots the English-Canadians or by the Dominion authorities.

Although French is a legal language in the Federal Parliament, the Separatists complain that it is not a compulsory subject for the admission to the Civil Service, so that much Federal business, even when it concerns Quebec, is carried out in English. They point out, too, that in Quebec itself hardly any large business firm appoints French-Canadians to its senior posts; the very director of personnel may be English though the firm employs thousands of French-speaking workers, who are thus debarred from presenting their grievances in their own language! They add that French government and business employees have to be not only English-speaking but English-thinking, so that instead of using their much valued French logic, they have to ' reason ' on pragmatic lines like the Anglo-Saxons.

Recently the Separatist feeling has intensified, partly through a resurgence of French-Canadian culture in the schools and universities and partly through world-wide political developments. If negro states like Sierra Leone can have a seat on the United Nations, if a small French-speaking country like Mali can be independent, the Separatists ask, why cannot Quebec, the home of an advanced civilisation and culture of European origin, and the second-largest French-speaking community in the world?

The modern Separatist movement is, however, the most recent upsurge of a long-standing resentment against British domination. If many French Canadians can feel so strongly now that this has lasted two hundred years, what must they have felt when it was still comparatively recent?

During the nineteenth century there were indeed a number of armed risings against English rule. Though of course fictitious, Verne's narrative is based upon that of 1837, and his deep sympathy for those whom he regarded as his own compatriots subjected to the yoke of ' perfidious Albion ' gives his writing its sincerity and force. We, too, without necessarily agreeing with him, can understand something of his feelings, for in our own time we have seen enough of Resistance Movements to appreciate their sincerity and idealism even though we do not approve of their aims.

Human nature being what it is, the struggle was bound to be marked by atrocities. By modern standards, however, these were comparatively few, and there was no organised campaign of terrorism; public opinion would not have tolerated that, and in those days public opinion still counted for something. The struggle also involved little in the way of reprisals; once the fighting was over the British Government was anxious to be conciliatory, to produce a settlement acceptable to both parties. Most of the French-Canadians, for their part, were only too thankful that peace was restored: British rule was preferable to an intermittent civil war.

Jules Verne's literary reputation rests partly on his adventure stories but chiefly on his work as a pioneer of science fiction. His achievements as a writer of historical fiction have almost been ignored; yet they well deserve recognition. In this field all his work has the general theme of subjugated peoples ' rightfully struggling to be free;' and among his historical stories *Family Without a Name* may well claim to be the best.

The second part of the narrative, which in the present edition is entitled *Into the Abyss,* describes the upshot of the struggle whose outbreak is dealt with here.

To my regret, I have been unable to find out who translated the Ode which appears in Chapter III; how admirably he has conveyed its spirit may be seen by comparison with the original, which is quoted in the Appendix.

I.O.E.

CHAPTER I

HISTORICAL BACKGROUND

' WE PITY the wretched human race, who for the sake of a few acres of ice are cutting one another's throats ' commented the philosophers towards the end of the eighteenth century. The reference was to Canada, for whose possession the French and English were at war.

Two years previously, when all America was claimed by the kings of Spain and Portugal, Francis I had exclaimed ' I'd like to see the clause in Adam's will which left them this vast heritage! ' And he had some reason for saying so, for part of this region was soon to take the name of New France.

The French, it is true, have not been able to keep this magnificent American colony. None the less, much of its population still remains French, and is attached to Ancient Gaul by those ties of blood, of racial identity, and of natural instinct, which international politics can never break. And those ' few acres of ice,' as they were contemptuously called, now form a Kingdom whose area is greater than that of Europe.

A Frenchman had taken possession of these vast territories in 1534. Jacques Cartier, of St. Malo, had followed deep into the heart of the country a river which he called the St. Lawrence. A year later another French explorer reached a group of log-huts—' Canada ' in the Indian language—which has become Quebec and

11

another hamlet which has become Montreal. Two centuries later these cities, about the same time as Kingston and Toronto both claimed to be capitals, until, to put an end to their rivalries, Ottawa was declared to be the centre of government of that great American colony which is now known as the Dominion of Canada.

In 1606 another Frenchman, Champlain, founded Quebec, and a few years later the English established their first settlements on the shores of Virginia. Then were sown the seeds of national jealousy which developed into a struggle between England and France in the New World. The Indians were drawn into it, the Algonquins and the Hurons siding with Champlain against the Iroquois, who allied themselves with the forces of the United Kingdom.

The war continued intermittently and with varying fortunes. It involved horrible massacres, and ended only when, after Wolfe and Montcalm had fallen on the Heights of Abraham, Louis XV, by the treaty of 1763, ceded to England all rights in the whole Canadian territory.

But the English did not understand how to conciliate the peoples who had submitted to them; they knew only how to destroy.* But a nationality cannot be destroyed when most of its inhabitants have kept the love of their former motherland and her ideals. In vain did the British try to impose English law on the French Canadians, to force them to take an oath of loyalty. As a result of energetic protests a Bill was passed in 1774 placing the colony under French legislation.

---

*It will be remembered that this account of the position in Canada is written from the point of view of a patriotic Frenchman! —I.O.E.

Now, having nothing further to fear from France, the United Kingdom found itself faced with the Americans. Their forces even marched upon Quebec, but did not succeed in storming the City. A year later—on 4th July 1776—came the Declaration of Independence of the United States.

Then came a distressing time for the French Canadians. The English were obsessed by one fear, that their colony would escape them by joining the great Federation and seeking refuge under the Star-Spangled Banner which the Americans were unfurling just over the horizon. But nothing of the sort happened—which is to be regretted in the interests of all true patriots.*

In 1791 a new Constitution divided the land into two provinces: Upper Canada in the west, Lower Canada in the east, with Quebec as its capital. But the struggle continued between the two races, at first solely on the political field. The royalists—the loyalists, as they called themselves—even thought of repealing the Constitution of 1791, and of reuniting Canada into one province, so as to give more influence to the British element, and to proscribe the use of the French language, which was still the language of parliament and judicature. But the ' reformist ' deputies protested so energetically that the Crown gave up this detestable scheme.

Yet the dispute became more embittered, and the election led to serious clashes: in 1831 a riot in Montreal cost the lives of three French-Canadian patriots. Meanwhile, thanks to emigration, the English element in Canada was reinforced, and became more audacious than ever; its only aim was to anglicise Lower Canada at all

---

*In this context the word ' patriot ' refers to a member of one of the French-Canadian ' reformists ' or to their sympathisers.—I.O.E.

costs. The patriots, on the other hand, had decided to resist, legally or otherwise. From so tense a situation, terrible conflicts might arise; the blood of both races would flow on a soil originally conquered by the courage of the French explorers.

Such was the position in 1837, when this record begins. It is essential to understand the antagonism between the French and the English, the vitality of the one, the tenacity of the other.

And yet was not that New France a fragment of *la patrie*, like Alsace and Lorraine, which were to be torn away thirty years later by a brutal invasion? And the efforts made by the French Canadians to regain at least their autonomy—is it not an example which the French of Alsace and Lorraine should never forget?

It was indeed to make arrangements in view of a probable insurrection that the Governor, Lord Gosford, the Commandant-general, Sir John Colborne, Colonel Gore and the Chief of Police, Gilbert Argall, were consulting together on the evening of 23rd August, 1837. The symptoms of a revolt were only too evident, and they had to be prepared for any emergency.

' How many men can you muster? ' Lord Gosford asked Sir John Colborne.

' Far too few, I regret to say,' the general replied, ' and I'll have to call in some of the troops from the country. I cannot bring into action more than forty battalions and seven companies of infantry, for we can't possibly withdraw any from the garrisons of the forts at Quebec and Montreal.'

' What artillery have you? '

' Three or four field-guns.'

' And cavalry? '

' Only a picket.'

' If you have to disperse those troops over the adjoining countryside,' Colonel Gore reflected, ' there won't be enough. It's very unfortunate that you had to dissolve the constitutional associations formed by the Loyalists. Then we should have had hundreds of volunteers, whose help we should not despise.'

' I could not let those associations continue,' Lord Gosford explained. ' Their contact with the people would have led to disturbances every day. We had to avoid everything that might have led to an explosion. We're on a powder-magazine, and we must walk in felt slippers.'

The governor was not exaggerating; he was a man of great ability, and a conciliatory disposition. Since his arrival in the colony he had shown much kindness to the French colonists, having—as was well said—' a dash of Irish gaiety, which harmonised very well with that of the Canadians.' If the rebellion had not yet broken out it was because of the circumspection, the kindness, the spirit of justice which Lord Gosford had shown; both by nature and by conviction he was opposed to violent measures.

' Force,' he said, ' may compress, but it does not suppress. In England they forget that Canada is next door to the United States, and that the United States ended by gaining their independence. I can see that in London the ministry wants an aggressive policy. By the advice of the Commissioners, Parliament has passed by a large majority a resolution to prosecute the opposition Deputies, to make use of the public funds, to alter the constitution so as to double the number of the English electors. But that does not show much wisdom: there'll be bloodshed on one side or the other.'

This was indeed to be feared. The steps taken by the British Parliament had produced an agitation which only wanted an opportunity to declare itself. Secret councils and public meetings were arousing public opinion. Threats were being exchanged at Montreal as at Quebec between the Reformists and the supporters of the English domination, and the police knew that a call to arms had been circulating throughout the country. The governor-general had been hanged in effigy. All they could do was to prepare for the outbreak.

' Has Monsieur de Vaudreuil been seen at Montreal? ' Lord Gosford asked.

' He doesn't seem to have left his house,' said Gilbert Argall. ' But his friends keep visiting him, and they're in daily touch with the liberal Deputies, and particularly with Gramont of Quebec.'

' If an outbreak occurs, it will undoubtedly be due to them,' Sir John Colborne agreed.

' Then why not arrest them? ' asked Colonel Gore. ' Why doesn't your lordship destroy the plot before it is hatched? '

' If it doesn't get hatched first! ' The Governor-general turned to the chief of the police. ' Didn't Monsieur de Vaudreuil and his friends take part in the insurrections of 1832 and 1835? '

' They did,' Sir Gilbert Argall replied, ' or rather there was good reason to think so; but direct proof was lacking, and it was impossible to prosecute them, just as it had been in 1825.'

' That proof should be obtained at any price,' Sir John Colborne declared, ' so that we might put a stop to the intrigues of these Reformists once and for all. There's nothing more hateful than civil war! But if it comes to that, we must show no mercy, and the struggle must end to the advantage of England.'

Such words were characteristic of the Commander-in-Chief of the British Forces in Canada. Sir John Colborne was the man to put down a revolution with all due vigour; yet to take part in secret investigations such as fall to the lot of the police would be not at all to his taste. Hence for many months police agents had had the whole of the task of watching the proceedings of the French-Canadian party. The towns and the parishes of the St. Lawrence valley had swarmed with detectives. At Montreal, in place of those constitutional bodies whose dissolution Colonel Gore regretted, the Doric Club—all its members were the most fanatical of loyalists—had taken upon itself to suppress the insurgents by all possible means. And Lord Gosford feared that at any moment, day or night, the outbreak might occur.

It can be understood, therefore, how the Governor's friends urged him to support the bureaucrats—as the supporters of the Crown were called—against those who upheld the national cause. Besides, Sir John Colborne was not the man for half-measures, as would appear later, when he succeeded Lord Gosford in the government of the colony. Colonel Gore, an old soldier and a hero of Waterloo was all for acting vigorously, and without delay.

On 7th May this year a meeting, in which the leading Reformists had taken part, had passed a number of resolutions, which were to become the political programme of the French Canadian opposition. Thus they proclaimed that ' Canada, like Ireland, should rally round a man endowed with a hatred of oppression, and a love of his country, which nothing, neither promises nor menaces, can shake.'

The man who said this was the Deputy Papineau, who had an immense popularity among the French-Canadians.

At the same time the assembly decided to abstain as much as possible from consuming imported articles, and only to use the country's own products, so as to deprive the government of the revenue obtained from the duties on foreign merchandise.

Lord Gosford replied to these declarations on 15th June, by a proclamation forbidding seditious meetings, and by ordering the magistrates and officers of the militia to disperse them.

But although Papineau was the ostensible leader, there was another who worked in the dark, and so mysteriously that the principal reformers had seldom seen him. Around this personage a legend had grown, and had given him extraordinary influence over the popular mind. Jean-Sans-Nom was the only name by which he was known.

' And this Jean-Sans-Nom,' asked Sir John Colborne; ' have you got on his track? '

' Not yet,' the chief of police replied. ' But I have reason to think that he's reappeared in Lower Canada, and that he has even been quite recently in Quebec.'

' And your men haven't been able to lay their hands on him! ' exclaimed Colonel Gore.

' That isn't too easy, General.'

' Has this man really got the influence they ascribe to him? ' Lord Gosford asked.

' Certainly,' Argall replied. ' I can assure your lordship that his influence is very great indeed.'

' Who is he? '

' That's what they all want to know,' said Sir John Colborne. ' That's right, isn't it, Argall? '

' That is so. Nobody knows who he is, whence he

comes, or whither he goes. He has appeared in this way, almost invisibly, in all the recent insurrections. There can be no doubt that Papineau and all the other leaders, expect him to strike when the time comes. Jean-Sans-Nom has become a sort of supernatural being among the people bordering the St. Lawrence above Montreal and below Quebec. If the legend is to be taken seriously, he has all the qualifications of a leader, extraordinary boldness, and a courage proof against anything. And, above all, there's the mystery of his incognito.'

' You think he's been in Quebec? ' asked Lord Gosford.

' The information I have received leads me to suppose so,' Argall explained. ' And I've put on his track all the smartest men I know, including that Rip who showed so much intelligence over the Morgaz affair.'

' Simon Morgaz,' said Sir John Colborne, ' that man who in 1825 so conveniently handed over his accomplices in the Chambly plot for a consideration? '

' The same.'

' Do you know what has become of him? '

' Only one thing,' said Argall, ' that he was boycotted by all the French Canadians whom he betrayed, and that he has vanished. He may have left America. He may be dead.'

' But might not what worked with Simon Morgaz work with these reformers? ' Sir John Colborne enquired.

' Don't think that, general! ' Lord Gosford replied. ' They're right above that sort of thing. That they are enemies of the English influence, and dream of obtaining for Canada the same independence as the United States, that's only too true. But to hope to buy them, to turn them into traitors by the promise of money or honours, that will never do! I don't think you'll find a single traitor amongst them.'

' They said the same of Simon Morgaz,' said Sir John Colborne ironically, ' and yet he betrayed his friends. And who knows if this Jean-Sans-Nom isn't to be sold? '

' I don't think so,' the chief of the police spoke in decided tones.

' Anyhow,' said Colonel Gore, ' whether he's to be sold or hanged, the first thing is to catch him, and if he's been seen at Quebec . . .'

At that moment a man appeared on one of the garden paths; he stopped about ten yards off. Argall recognised the policeman, or rather the police agent, for the newcomer did not belong to the regular forces.

' That's Rip, of Rip and Co.,' he told Lord Gosford. ' Your lordship will allow me to hear what he has to say? '

As Lord Gosford nodded, Rip approached respectfully, and waited for Argall to ask:

' Have you made sure that Jean-Sans-Nom has been seen in Quebec? '

' I have, your honour! '

' And why wasn't he arrested? ' asked Lord Gosford.

' Your lordship must excuse my associates and myself,' Rip explained, ' but we didn't get warning in time. The day before yesterday we heard that Jean-Sans-Nom had visited one of the houses in the Rue de Petit-Champlain, next to the tailor's shop. I surrounded the house, which is occupied by Sebastien Gramont, Advocate and Deputy, who's very prominent in the Reformist party. But Jean-Sans-Nom was not there, although Gramont has certainly had dealings with him. All our enquiries were in vain.'

'Do you think the man is still in Quebec?' asked Sir John Colborne.

'I cannot say definitely, your Excellency.'

'You don't know him?'

'I've never seen him, and indeed there are very few who have.'

'Do you know which way he went when he left Quebec?'

'I do not.'

'And what do you think?' asked the Minister of Police.

'My idea is that he has gone towards Montreal, where the agitators seem to be concentrating. If an insurrection is being planned it is in that part of Lower Canada that it is likely to break out. I suspect that Jean-Sans-Nom is lying low in some village on the bank of the St. Lawrence.'

'And that,' Argall commented, 'is where we ought to look.'

'Well, give the necessary orders,' said the Governor.

'Your lordship shall be satisfied. Rip, tomorrow you will leave Quebec with the best men you have. I'll watch Monsieur de Vaudreuil and his friends, who are certainly in touch with Jean-Sans-Nom. Try and get on his track by any means. It is the Governor-General's express order.'

'And it will be faithfully obeyed,' said Rip. 'I'll go tomorrow.'

'We approve in advance,' Gilbert Argall continued, 'of anything you think necessary to effect the capture of this dangerous fellow. We want him dead or alive, before he can raise the French-Canadians by his presence. You are intelligent and zealous, Rip; you showed that a dozen years ago in the Morgaz affair. We reckon once more on your zeal and intelligence. You may go.

Rip was preparing to leave, and had already taken a few steps backward when he stopped.

' May I ask your honour one question? ' he asked.

' A question? ' said Argall.

' Yes, your honour, for it has to be settled, so that the books of Rip and Co. can be kept in proper order.'

' What is it? '

' Is there a price on Jean-Sans-Nom's head? '

' Not yet! '

' There ought to be! ' said Sir John Colborne.

' There is,' Lord Gosford decided.

' What is the amount? ' asked Rip.

' Four thousand dollars.'

' It's worth six thousand,' said Rip. ' I shall have to pay for travelling and other special expenses.'

' Very well,' Lord Gosford agreed.

' It will be money your lordship will never regret.'

' If it is earned . . .' added the minister.

' It will be, your honour! '

And with this promise—a rather hazardous one, per-haps—the senior partner in Rip and Co. retired.

' This Rip seems to know what he is about,' said Colonel Gore.

' And he gives us confidence in him,' said Argall. ' This reward of six thousand dollars will improve his skill and his zeal. That Chambly affair brought him something considerable, and though he's fond of his work, he's fonder still of the cash it brings him. You must take him as he is, and I don't know anyone more likely to catch Jean-Sans-Nom, if Jean-Sans-Nom will let himself be caught! '

The others took leave of Lord Gosford. Then Sir John Colborne instructed Colonel Gore to set out at once for Montreal, where his colleague, Colonel Wetherall, was waiting, with orders to prevent, as much as possible, the spread of the insurrection.

CHAPTER II

TWELVE YEARS EARLIER

SIMON MORGAZ! A name execrated in the lowliest huts of Canada! A name held up for long years to public execration! Simon Morgaz! The traitor who had betrayed his brothers, and sold his country.

In 1825—twelve years before the 1837 insurrection—a few French Canadians had organized a conspiracy, whose object was to free Canada from the English domination which weighed on it so heavily. They were bold men, active, energetic, of good position, and sprung, for the most part, from the early immigrants, who had founded New France. No wonder that they could not believe that their colony had been permanently handed over to England. And even admitting that the country could never return to the descendants of Cartier and Champlain, had it not the right to its independence? And it was to gain its independence that they were to risk their lives.

Amongst them was Monsieur de Vaudreuil, a descendant of the old governors of Canada under Louis XIV—one of those families whose French names have become geographical names in the Dominion's cartography.

His associates were, like himself, of French origin, although marriages with Anglo-American families had changed their French names. Thanks either to their

24

birth or to their wealth they exercised a great influence over the people of town and country.

The real leader of the conspiracy was Walter Hodge, who was of American nationality. Although he was then sixty, age had not cooled the heat of his blood. During the War of Independence he had been one of those daring volunteers known as "skinners" whose wild violence Washington had to tolerate, because of the vigour with which they harassed the Royal Army. At the end of the eighteenth century, Canada had been incited by the United States to enter the American federation; this explains why an American like Walter Hodge should have joined this conspiracy, and even become its leader. He was one of those who had adopted as his motto the four words which summarise the Monroe doctrine, "America for the Americans."

Walter Hodge and his companions had never ceased from protesting against the exactions of the English administration, which became more and more intolerable. In 1822 their names figured in the protest against the union of Upper and Lower Canada, and they fought with pen and speech against the iniquitous way in which the country was being shared among the bureaucrats so as to strengthen the English element. They had attacked all the governors, and associated themselves in every way with the opposition deputies.

In 1825, however, the conspiracy had a definite object, and was organized without reference to the Liberals of the Canadian Assembly. If Papineau and his colleagues were not admitted to its secrets, Hodge could count on them to make certain of its results if they succeeded.

At the outset it was intended to seize upon the person of Lord Dalhousie, who in 1820 had been nominated to the post of Governor-General of the English colonies in North America. On his arrival, he seemed to have decided upon a policy of concession. Thanks to him, the Roman Catholic Archbishop of Quebec was officially recognised and Montreal, Rose, and Regiopolis became new bishoprics.

Still, however, the British Cabinet had refused Canada the right of self-government. The members of the Legislative Council, nominated for life by the Crown, were all English by birth, and overruled the House of Assembly elected by the people. Out of a population of 600,000 inhabitants, including 525,000 French Canadians, three-quarters of the government officials were of English descent. And the question had again been mooted of proscribing the legal use of the French language throughout the colony.

To thwart this, nothing else could succeed but an act of violence. To seize on Lord Dalhousie and the principal members of the Legislative Council and then, this *coup d'état* effected, to provoke a popular movement along the St. Lawrence, to instal a provisional government until an election had brought into being a National Government, and to raise the Canadian Militia against the Regular Army, such were the plans of Walter Hodge and his associates.

With them was also associated a certain Simon Morgaz, who in 1825 was forty-six years old. A lawyer in a country where there are more lawyers than clients, just as there are more doctors than patients, he lived rather frugally at Chambly, a dozen leagues from Montreal.

He was a resolute man, whose energy had attracted attention when the Reformists protested against the proceedings of the British Cabinet. His pleasant manner and prepossessing face made him generally liked. No one imagined that the personality of a traitor would one day appear behind so attractive a façade.

Simon Morgaz was married and his wife was eight years younger than he, being then thirty-eight. Of American origin, she was the daughter of Major Allen, whose bravery during the War of Independence may be appreciated from the fact that he was one of Washington's aide-de-camps. A personification of loyalty, he would have surrendered his life to keep his word with the calmness of a Regulus.

It was at Albany, in New York State, that the two had met. The young lawyer was a French Canadian, as Major Allen well knew—for he would never have given his daughter to the descendant of an English family. Although Morgaz had no personal fortune, yet what came to Bridget on the death of her mother would assure the young couple a certain comfort, if not wealth. The marriage took place at Albany in 1806.

Morgaz and his wife might have been happy, but they were not. Not that Morgaz ever failed in his care for his wife, for whom he always entertained a sincere affection, but a passion devoured him—a passion for gambling. Bridget's patrimony was dissipated in a few years, and although her husband was recognised as a lawyer of talent, his work did not suffice to fill up the gaps in his fortune. It was not poverty but penury that his wife had to bear. Bridget never reproached her husband; her advice having been useless, she accepted the trial with resignation and with courage, although her future was full of anxiety.

It was not only for herself that Bridget had to fear. During the first years of her married life she had had two children, to whom she had given the same baptismal name, with a slight variation. The elder, Joann, was born in 1807; the younger, Jean, in 1808, and Bridget devoted herself entirely to her sons' education. Joann was of a gentle disposition; Jean of a more lively temperament, though beneath their gentleness and vivacity both were energetic enough. They plainly took after their mother, having serious minds, a taste for work, and a straight-forward way of looking at things, which was certainly lacking in Simon Morgaz. To their father they were always respectful, but there was none of that natural ease and unreserved confidence which is the very essence of blood relationship. For their mother their devotion was unbounded, their affection overflowing. Bridget and her sons were united by a double chain of love which nothing could ever break.

After their childhood, Joann and Jean had been sent to school at Chambly, where they gained the reputation of being among the foremost pupils in the junior division. When they were respectively twelve and thirteen they had gone to Montreal College, where they soon came to the front. Two years elapsed, and they had just finished their education when there came the events of 1825.

Though Simon Morgaz and his wife usually resided at Montreal, where the lawyer's office was in daily danger of having to close down, they had managed to retain possession of a small house at Chambly. It was there that Walter Hodge and his friends had met, when Morgaz had entered the plot whose first act would be the arrest of the Governor-General, and its next the appointment of a provisional government at Quebec.

Under this modest roof in the village of Chambly the conspirators believed they were in greater safety than they would have been at Montreal, where the police surveillance was very keen. Yet they acted with great prudence, so as to throw all attempts at espionage off the scent. Arms and ammunition had been stored in the house without their transport evoking the least suspicion. And it was from Chambly, where the threads of the plot were spun, that the signal was to be given.

But the Governor got wind of the plot, and on the evening of 25th August the house of Simon Morgaz was entered by the police, who were led by Rip, just as the conspirators had met. There was no time to destroy their secret correspondence, or to burn the lists of their supporters, and the police seized the arms hidden in the cellars. The plot was revealed, and Simon Morgaz, Vaudreuil, and a dozen others were taken to Montreal under a strong escort.

There was then at Quebec a certain Rip, who kept a private inquiry and detective office, and who was often employed on government business, not without a consideration. To him a police investigation was merely a matter of cash, and he passed it through his books like a merchant, charging so much for the job—so much for a search, so much for an arrest, so much for espionage. He was a very shrewd man, very keen, very daring, and enough of a man of the world to have his hand—or rather his nose—in everybody's business. What is more, he was quite devoid of scruples, and had not the shadow of a moral sense.

In 1825, Rip, who had just started his agency, was thirty-three years of age. Already his cleverness in disguises had enabled him to have a hand in several affairs under different names. For some years he had known Simon Morgaz, with whom he had had business in legal matters. Certain circumstances which would have appeared insignificant to anyone else made him think that the advocate of Montreal was concerned in some way with the conspiracy at Chambly. He kept a watch on him; he pried into the secrets of his private life; he frequented the house, although Bridget took no pains to hide the antipathy she felt for him.

A letter seized at the post office confirmed the lawyer's complicity. The minister of police, informed of this result of his inquiries, advised Rip to act judiciously with Morgaz, whom he knew to be in pecuniary difficulties; at last the detective suddenly gave the unhappy man the choice between two alternatives—to be prosecuted for treason, or to receive the enormous sum of a hundred thousand piastres, or dollars, the value being the same, for revealing the names of his accomplices and the details of the conspiracy at Chambly.

The advocate was astounded. . . Betray his companions! Sell them for gold! Hand them over to the scaffold! Yet he succumbed; he accepted the price of his treason, he revealed the secrets of the conspirators, after receiving a promise that his infamy would never be divulged. It was even agreed that the police should arrest him at the same time as Walter Hodge and his friends, that he should be tried by the same judges, and that he should be sentenced—and it could only be a sentence of death—and that he should then be allowed to escape.

This abominable scheme was concocted between the minister of police, the head partner of Rip and Co., and Simon Morgaz.

Things happened as had been arranged. On the day named by the traitor, the conspirators were surprised in the house of Chambly, and on 25th September, 1825, they were all tried together.

The only reply the prisoners made to the charge was to attack the British ministry. To the legal arguments they answered only with arguments of the purest patriotism. Did they not realise that they were condemned in advance, that nothing could save them?

The trial lasted for several hours, and all would have gone as arranged, had not something revealed the conduct of Simon Morgaz.

One of the witnesses declared that he had frequently seen the lawyer conferring with Rip. It was a flash of revelation. Walter Hodge and Vaudreuil, who for some time had been suspicious of Morgaz because of his strange behaviour, saw their suspicions confirmed by this evidence. The conspiracy had been carried on so secretly, and had been so easily discovered, that it was obvious that some traitor had been at work. Rip was examined and plied with questions, to which he could not reply without embarrassment. Simon Morgaz tried to defend himself; but he launched forth into such improbabilities and such unconvincing explanations, that his comrades and even his judges soon realised the truth. A scoundrel had betrayed his accomplices, and that traitor was Simon Morgaz.

An irresistible feeling of repulsion arose among the prisoners and the public who crowded the court.

'President of the Court,' said Walter Hodge, ' we demand that Simon Morgaz be removed from this dock, which is honoured by our presence, and dishonoured by his. We do not wish to be contaminated any longer by contact with this man.'

The other prisoners joined Hodge who, unable to

restrain himself, had attacked Morgaz, and to whose rescue the warders had to come. The President of the Court ordered Morgaz to be taken back to prison. Howls accompanied him; the threats he heard told him he was looked upon as a traitor, whose treason would cost him his life at the hands of the more fervent apostles of Canadian independence. Walter Hodge and two others were declared to be the leaders of the Chambly conspiracy, and sentenced to death. On the next day, 27th September, after another appeal to their people's patriotism, they died on the scaffold.

The other accused, among whom was M. de Vaudreuil, whether they seemed to be less compromised, or whether the Government wished to inflict the capital punishment only on the leaders, were allowed to escape with their lives. Sentenced to imprisonment for life, they did not receive their liberty till 1829, when a general amnesty was granted to political offenders.

What became of Simon Morgaz after the execution? Allowed to leave the prison at Montreal, he hastened to disappear.

But universal reprobation weighed on his name, and in consequence it fell on those who were in no way responsible for his treason. Bridget Morgaz was brutally hunted from the house she occupied at Montreal, and from the cottage at Chambly, where she had sought refuge while the proceedings were in progress. She took with her her two sons, who had been hunted from college, as their father had been hunted from the dock in the court of justice.

Where had Simon Morgaz decided to hide his unworthy existence, when his wife and children joined him a few days later? In a distant village a long way from Montreal.

But Bridget did not believe that her husband was guilty, nor did Joann nor Jean. The four retired to the village of Verchères, on the bank of the St. Lawrence. Here, they hoped, no suspicion would expose them to the public scorn. They lived miserably on the resources which remained to them, for Simon, although he had received the reward for his treason, took care not to use it before his wife and sons. In their presence he always protested his innocence, and he cursed the injustice which had fallen on his family and on himself. If he had been a traitor, would he not have the price of his treason to support him? Would he have thus been reduced to penury?

And Bridget inferred that her husband was guiltless, and she rejoiced at this, for it gave the lie to his enemies. Appearances were against him. He could not explain them. He was the victim of a horrible combination of circumstances. Some day he would be justified. He was innocent!

As regards his two sons a difference was observable in their attitude towards their father. The eldest, Joann, kept himself aloof, and did not dare to think of the opprobrium which had thus fallen on the name of Morgaz. The arguments for and against rose before his mind, and he rejected them as impossible to fathom. He would not be his father's judge, so much did he fear that the verdict would go against him. He shut his eyes, he kept silent, he held himself aloof when his mother and his brother would have reasoned with him. The wretched boy obviously feared that he would have to find guilty the man whose son he was.

Jean's attitude, on the other hand, was quite different. He believed in the innocence of the alleged conspirators, although the presumptions against them were overwhelming. More impetuous than Joann, less master of his own judgment, he let himself be carried away by his instincts of filial affection. He would have defended his father publicly. When he heard people talk of Simon Morgaz, his heart bounded, and his mother had to interfere to prevent an outburst. Thus did the unfortunate family live at Verchères under an assumed name, and in complete moral and material poverty. And with what fury the people of the village would have risen against them, had their real name been known!

But the people of Verchères soon began to get uneasy about this family, whose origin they did not know, whose life was so mysterious; and though their incognito was never betrayed, suspicion arose against them. One morning the word ' Traitor ' was found written on their door.

Next morning Morgaz and his family went away. Crossing the St. Lawrence, they stayed for a few days in one of the villages on the left bank of the river. There attention was directed to them, and they left that village. They were now wanderers, hated by all. Vengeance, it might be said, blazing torch in hand, pursued them, as, in the Biblical story, she had pursued the murderer of Abel. Morgaz and his family could settle nowhere. They set out towards the east, towards the less-inhabited regions, but wherever they went their name was thrown in their face.

Two months after the trial, the family had fled beyond Ontario. Near Kingston they were recognised at an inn, and had to leave at once, Simon having only just time to escape during the night. In vain Bridget and Jean wanted to defend him. They scarcely got away themselves without being ill-treated, and Joann might have been killed as he covered their retreat.

They met again on the borders of a lake, a few miles beyond Kingston. They went along its southern shore to enter the United States, for refuge could no longer be found even in Upper Canada, though this region was not yet affected by the reformist ideals. Yet would not the same welcome await them on the other side of the frontier, where the people of the United States had had some experience of traitors? Better to reach some lost country, some Indian tribe. It was in vain. The unhappy man was driven away everywhere. Everywhere he was recognised, as if he bore on his forehead a mark which exposed him to public infamy.

It was the end of November. What weary travelling in this fearful weather, in the glacial winds and the rigorous cold of the winter season in the lake country. As they journeyed through the villages, the sons bought a little food, while the father kept in hiding. They slept, when they could, in abandoned huts, or when these failed, in the clefts of the rocks, or under the trees of the interminable forests that covered the land.

Simon Morgaz became ever more gloomy and savage. He never stopped exculpating himself before his family, as if some invisible accuser were following in his tracks and shouting ' Traitor! traitor! ' And now he seemed unable to look his wife and children in the face. Bridget tried to comfort him with affectionate words, and though Joann kept silence, Jean never ceased to protest.

' Father, father! ' he would say, ' don't let yourself give in! Time will do justice on your slanderers. They will see that they have been deceived, that appearances were against you! You to have betrayed your comrades, to have sold your country! '

'No, no!' Simon would reply, but in so feeble a voice that it was almost inaudible.

The family, wandering from village to village, at last reached the western end of the lake, a few miles from Fort Toronto. They had only to get to the river Niagara where it enters the lake, to cross over to the American bank.

Was it there that Morgaz meant to stop? Would it not be better to go further west, to reach a country so distant that the rumour of his infamy had not spread to it? But where was he to go? His wife and sons did not know, for he always led the way, and all they had to do was to follow.

On 3rd December, in the evening, exhausted with fatigue and privations, they had halted in a cave half hidden by brushwood and briars—doubtless some abandoned lair of the wild beasts. The little food that remained to them had been put down on the sand. Bridget had succumbed to physical and mental weariness. At any cost, Morgaz must find in the nearest village some Indian tribe who, for a few days, would grant the hospitality which the Canadians never refuse.

Joann and Jean, tortured with hunger, were eating some cold venison. But neither Simon nor Bridget could eat anything.

'Father,' said Jean, 'you must recruit your strength.'

Simon Morgaz made no reply.

'Father,' said Joann, and this was the first time he had spoken to him since they had left Chambly, 'we cannot go any further! Mother cannot stand any more travelling. Here we are on the American frontier; are you going to cross it?'

Simon looked at his eldest son, and his eyes dropped almost at once. Joann continued:

' Look at the state mother is in. She cannot move! This torpor is going to rob her of all the energy she has left! Tomorrow she won't be able to get up. My brother and I can go on, no doubt! But we must know where you are going. What is it you mean to do? '

Smion Morgaz did not reply. He bowed his head, and went to the back of the cave.

Night fell. No sound disturbed the solitude. Thick clouds covered the sky and threatened to fall in a dense mist. Except for the howls of some distant wild beast not a breath disturbed the atmosphere. Heavy flakes of snow began to fall. The cold was intense, so Jean gathered some dead wood and lit a fire in a corner, where the smoke would drift outwards.

Bridget, stretched on a bed of grass that Joann had gathered, lay motionless. The little life that remained to her was only revealed by her painful breathing, broken by long and sorrowful sighs. While Joann held her hand, Jean fed the fire.

Simon Morgaz lay, half-crouching in the darkness, in an attitude of despair, as if he were horror-stricken at himself, as was shown when the reflection of the fire occasionally lit up his face.

Then the firelight gradually sank, and in spite of himself, Jean felt his eyes closing.

How long did he remain asleep? He did not know. He could not say. But when he awoke, the fire was nearly out.

He rose and threw an armful of wood on the fire, which he rekindled with his breath so that the cavern was once more lit up.

Bridget and Joann, huddled together, were still motionless. But Simon Morgaz was no longer there! Why had he left the place where his wife and sons were asleep?

Gripped by a dreadful presentiment, Jean was rushing out of the cave when he heard an explosion.

Bridget and Joann leapt to their feet. They too had heard the explosion, which seemed to come from close by.

With a shriek of terror, Bridget staggered to her feet, and her sons helped her out of the cave.

They had not gone twenty paces when they saw a corpse lying on the snow.

It was the body of Simon Morgaz. He had shot himself in the heart. He was dead.

Joann and Jean recoiled, overwhelmed. The past rose before them. Was it true that their father was guilty? Or rather, had he in an excess of despair put an end to an existence he had found too hard to endure?

Bridget threw herself on her husband's body. She clasped it in her arms. She could not believe in the infamy of the man whose name she bore.

Joann raised his mother and took her back to the cave. Then he and his brother brought their father's body back to the place where it had lain a few hours before. A pocket-book slipped out on to the ground. Joann picked it up, and when he opened it, a roll of bank-notes fell out. It was the reward for which Simon Morgaz had betrayed the leaders of the Chambly conspiracy. The mother and the two sons could no longer doubt.

Joann and Jean knelt at Bridget's side.

And now, beside the corpse of the traitor who had done justice on himself, there now remained only a dishonoured family, whose name must die with him who had dishonoured it.

CHAPTER III

A HURON LAWYER

IT WAS not without good reason that the Governor and his advisers had been conferring regarding the measures to be taken for the repression of the Reformists. A formidable insurrection of the French Canadians was indeed about to take place.

But if Lord Gosford and his staff had good reason to be concerned, nothing seemed to trouble a certain young fellow, who, on the morning of 3rd September, was supposed to be ' engrossing ' in the office of Mr. Nick, in Bon Secours market-place, Montreal. ' Engrossing ' is not quite the word, perhaps, to apply to the absorbing occupation in which the clerk, Lionel Restigouche, was then employed at nine in the morning. A column of irregular lines, neatly written, extended down a fine sheet of bluish paper, which in no way resembled the parchment of a deed. At times, when Lionel's hand stopped while an idea took shape, his eyes looked listlessly out of the half-opened window towards the Nelson column in Jacques Cartier Place. Then his expression would liven up, and his pen resume its course, while he gently swayed his head as if beating time to some regular rhythm.

Lionel was barely seventeen. His face, still almost feminine, was French in type, and had a very pleasant expression; his hair was light and rather long, perhaps, and his eyes were as blue as the water in the Great Lakes.

Though he had neither father nor mother, Mr. Nick might be said to be both to him, for the estimable lawyer was as fond of him as if he had been his own son.

Lionel was alone in the office. There was nobody with him, not any of the other clerks, who were out on business, not even a client, although Mr. Nick's office was one of the busiest in the town. And Lionel, feeling sure he would not be interrupted, was taking his ease, and he had just signed his name with a wonderful flourish below the last line on his page, when he heard himself spoken to:

' What are you doing there, my boy? '

It was Mr. Nick, who had entered without Lionel's noticing him, so absorbed had he been in his unofficial work.

Lionel's first movement was to slip the paper in question under the blotting-pad, but the notary snatched away the suspicious document before the clerk could stop him.

' What is this, Lionel? ' he asked. ' An agreement? An engrossment? A copy of a contract? '

' Mr. Nick, believe me . . .'

The notary had put on his spectacles, and, his brows knitted, he scanned the page in astonishment. ' What is this? ' he exclaimed. ' Lines all unequal! Margin all down one side! Margin on the other! So much good ink wasted, so much good paper wasted by these useless margins! '

' Mr. Nick,' answered Lionel, blushing to the ears, ' that came to me—by chance . . .'

' What came to you—by chance? '

' The verses.'

' The verses! You write your drafts in verse, do you? Is not prose enough for you to draught a deed in? '

' That isn't a deed, if you please.'

' What is it, then? '

' It's a piece of poetry I've composed for the meeting of the Lyre-Amicale.'

' The Lyre-Amicale! ' exclaimed the notary. ' Do you imagine, Lionel, that it was for you to figure at the meeting of the Lyre-Amicale, or any other Parnassian conversazione, that I took you into my office? Was it for you to abandon yourself to these versifying gymnastics that I made you my clerk? Would it not have been better for you to spend your time canoeing on the St. Lawrence, or showing off your dandyism along the paths of Mont Royal or the Saint Hélène Park! Indeed! A poet in a notary's office! A clerk's head with a halo round it! Why, it's enough to frighten clients away! '

' Please don't be angry, Mr. Nick,' Lionel spoke in a piteous tone. ' If you only knew how our melodious French language lends itself to verse! It lends itself so nobly to rhythm, cadence, and harmony. Our poets . . .'

' Our poets do not fulfil the important functions of clerk that I know of. They are not paid—to say nothing of board and lodging—six dollars a month, and by me! They do not have to draw up contracts or wills, and they can Pindarize as much as they like! '

' Mr. Nick—this time . . .'

' Yes, this time you hoped to become the laureate of the Lyre-Amicale? '

' I did so foolishly presume . . .'

' And may I ask what is the subject of this effusion? Probably some dithyrambic evocation to Tabellionope, the muse of the Perfect Lawyer! '

' No,' Lionel made a gesture of protest.

' Then what do you call your rhymes? '

' *Will-o'-the-wisp.*'

' *Will-o'-the-wisp*! ' exclaimed Mr. Nick. ' Do you address verses to Will-o'-the-wisps? '

And probably the notary would have held forth on jinns, elves, brownies, goblins, water-sprites, and all the poetic figures of Scandinavian mythology, when the postman knocked at the door and appeared on the threshold.

' Ah! is that you, my friend? ' said Mr. Nick. ' I took you for a will-o'-the-wisp.'

' A will-o'-the-wisp, Mr. Nick? ' asked the postman. ' Do I look like one? '

' No; you look more like a postman who's brought me a letter.'

' Here it is, Mr. Nick.'

' Thank you! '

The postman retired just as, having caught sight of the handwriting, the lawyer at once opened the letter.

Lionel picked up his sheet of paper and put it in his pocket.

Mr. Nick read the letter very carefully; then he put it back in the envelope and looked at the postmark. The postmark was that of St. Charles, a small village in Verchères County, and the date was that of the previous day, 2nd September. After a minute's thought, the lawyer returned to his philippic against the poets.

' Ah, you worship the muses, Lionel? Well, as a punishment, you will accompany me to Laval, and you'll have time on the road to hammer out your verses.'

' Hammer them out, Mr. Nick? '

' We must be off in an hour, and if we meet any will-o'-the-wisps, you can do the polite to them.'

With that the lawyer when into his private office, while Lionel prepared for the journey, which he did not find unpleasing. Perhaps he might succeed in giving his employer more accurate ideas about poetry in general and on the sons of Apollo—even when they're lawyer's clerks.

An excellent man was Mr. Nick, and much appreciated for the accuracy of his judgment and the value of his advice. He was then about fifty; his engaging expression, his large smiling face surrounded by a cluster of curly hair which had once been very black, but was now turning grey; his quick, cheerful eyes, his splendid teeth, his laughing lips, his pleasant manners, all went to form a very sympathetic personality. One further detail: under Mr. Nick's well-tanned skin it could be seen that Indian blood flowed in his veins.

This was so, and the lawyer did not seek to hide it. He was descended from the old natives of the country, those who possessed the soil before any Europeans had crossed the ocean to conquer it. There had been many marriages between the French and the Indians, and some leading Frenchmen even became the chiefs of Indian tribes.

Nick by descent was a Huron; that is to say, he came from one of the four chief families of the Indian race. Although he could have borne the resounding name of Nicholas Sagamore, he was always known as Mr. Nick, and he was quite content with this.

His race was not extinct. One of his innumerable cousins was chief of the Redskins, and reigned over a Huron tribe in the north of Laprairie county, west of Montreal.

There is nothing strange about this in Canada. Quebec can boast many a worthy citizen whose birthright it is to brandish the tomahawk, and shout the war-cry of an Iroquois tribe. Happily, Mr. Nick did not belong to those perfidious Indians who have sided with the oppressors.

No! Descended from the Hurons, who almost always supported the French, he had nothing to blush for. And Lionel, too, was proud of his master, the undoubted descendant of the great chiefs of North America, and he only waited for an opportunity to celebrate his deeds in verse.

At Montreal Mr. Nick, neither a French-Canadian nor an Anglo-American, had always preserved a prudent neutrality between the two political parties. And, as everybody respected him, everybody had recourse to his services. Any hereditary tendencies he might have, seemed to have undergone a complete change. Never had the warlike dreams of his face revived in him. He was only a lawyer—a perfect lawyer—placid and conciliating. And he seemed to have no desire to perpetuate the name of the Sagamores, for he had never taken a wife, and never thought of taking one.

Mr. Nick was preparing to leave the office in company with his second clerk. He would only be away a few hours, and his old servant Dolly would keep dinner waiting for him.

Montreal has become a great city. In its west lies the English quarter and that of the Scots, known locally as the ' short petticoats '; in the east is the French quarter. The two races are the less inclined to mingle as nearly all the trade is in the hands of merchants of British origin, and this was even more true in 1837. That magnificent waterway, the St. Lawrence, assured the town's prosperity, putting it in communication not only with the rest of Canada, but also with Europe.

Mr. Nick was very well off. But he was one of the old school of lawyers, whose horizon is bounded by the four walls of their office, and who justify their claim to keep records by watching night and day over the contracts, minutes, and family papers confided to their care. So the descendant of the Sagamores lived in the old house on the Bon Secours market-place; and it was thence that, on the morning of 3rd September, he set out with his second clerk to find a vehicle for his journey.

The vehicle he hailed was one of those two-horse affairs which the Canadians call 'buggies.' They are a kind of coach, hung on springs, as comfortable as possible, but very strong, and suited to the hardness of the roads. They can hold half-a-dozen travellers.

'Eh! Mr. Nick!' exclaimed the driver of the buggy, as he caught sight of the lawyer, who was always greeted with this cordial exclamation.

'I myself, along with my clerk!' Mr. Nick replied with his habitual good-humour.

'Are you all right, Mr. Nick?'

'Yes, Tom, and you ought to try and be as well as I am. You wouldn't ruin yourself with physic . . .'

'Nor with physicians,' added Tom.

'When do we start?' asked Mr. Nick.

'Now.'

'Anyone going with us?'

'No one yet,' Tom replied, 'but someone may turn up at the last moment.'

'I hope so! I hope so, Tom! I like to talk as I travel, and when you want to talk I've noticed that it's as well not to be alone.'

Mr. Nick's wishes were apparently not to be satisfied this time. The horses were harnessed and Tom cracked his whip, but no traveller appeared.

The lawyer took the end seat, and Lionel sat down beside him; Tom gave a last look round, up and down

the road, and then he mounted the box, gathered up the
reins, whistled to his horses, and the noisy affair began
to move, just as some passers-by, who knew Nick—and
who did not know him, the worthy man?—wished him
a pleasant journey, to which he replied by a wave with
his hand.

The buggy went away uphill, towards Mont Royal.
The lawyer looked to right and left with as much care
as the driver, but for a different reason. Nobody seemed
to be that morning going to the north of the island for
him to have a chat with.

The vehicle had reached the circular promenade, and
the horses were breaking into a trot, when a man waved
the driver to stop. He sat down on the seat in front of
Lionel, having first greeted Mr. Nick and his clerk. The
buggy went off at a gentle trot, and a few minutes later
was out of sight of the galvanized iron roofs of the houses
of the town, which were shining in the sun like so many
silvered mirrors.

The lawyer had seen the newcomer enter the vehicle
with the most lively satisfaction. Now he could talk for
the twelve miles that separated Montreal from the upper
branch of the St. Lawrence. But the traveller seemed in
no mood in indulge in polite conversation. He had
glanced at Mr. Nick and Lionel, and then settled down
in a corner, and. with his eyes half closed, he seemed to
be absorbed in his reflections.

He was a young man, about twenty-nine years of age.
With his slight figure, his energetic face, his resolute look,
his manly features, his high forehead, and his dark hair,
he was a typical French-Canadian. What was he? Where
did he come from? Mr. Nick, who knew everybody, did
not know him, and had never seen him before. Looked at

closely, the young man seemed to have passed through much trouble, and to have been educated in the school of misfortune.

That the unknown belonged to the party agitating for national independence was obvious even from his dress, which was almost that of a backwoodsman. The cap he wore was a blue bonnet; buttoned across his chest was a sort of cape; and his trousers were of some coarse grey stuff, with a red sash round his waist. All the material was of local origin; the exclusive use of such material was in itself a political protest, as it excluded manufactured products imported from England. It was one of the thousand ways of defying the home authorities, and it was not without precedent—the Boston Tea-party.

Mr. Nick, however, as a neutral, wore trousers of Canadian make, and an overcoat of cloth imported from England. But, in the patriotic clothing worn by Lionel there was not as much as a thread woven beyond the Atlantic.

The buggy rolled along over the rough road of Montreal Island, and long did the journey seem to Mr. Nick, who was naturally so loquacious. But, as the young man did not seem disposed to begin, Mr. Nick turned on Lionel in the hope that their travelling companion would end by joining in the conversation.

' Well, Lionel,' began he, ' and how about this will-o'-the wisp? '

' The will-o'-the-wisp? ' asked the clerk.

' Yes! I've got tired of looking for it, and so far I haven't seen it.'

' There's too much daylight, perhaps,' Lionel kept up the joke.

' Perhaps if we sang the old song—

' Come along cheerily, goblin queer!

Come along cheerily, neighbour dear! '

But no—the goblin won't answer. By-the-bye, Lionel, you know how to get away from the blandishments of will-o'-the-wisps? '

' Certainly, Mr. Nick. All you have to do is to ask them what day of the month Christmas is; and, as they don't know, you have time to escape while they're thinking out an answer.'

' I see you know the traditions. Well, until one of that sort gets in our way, suppose we say something about the one you've got in your pocket? '

Lionel blushed slightly.

' You really want me to? '

' Yes, my boy! It will pass a quarter of an hour or so.'

Then the lawyer turned to the other passenger—

' You don't object to a little verse, sir? '

' Not at all,' the passenger assured him.

' It's a piece of poetry that my clerk has composed for the meeting of the Lyre-Amicale. These fellows fight shy of nothing! Come on, my young poet, present your piece —as the gunners say! '

Lionel was only too pleased to have a listener who might be more indulgent than Mr. Nick. So he produced his paper and began to read:

' THE WILL-O'-THE-WISP '

' A wayward flame that none can reach,

That doth its nightly guard deceive,

And in the darkening hours of eve,

Nor on the wave, nor on the beach,

A trace behind doth leave.

'A flame so quick to fade and flee,
In purple oft, and oft in white!
To solve this mystery of light,
The will-o'-the-wisp pursued must be
And captured in its flight.'

'Yes,' said Mr. Nick; 'captured, and put in a cage!
Go on, Lionel '—

'Is it a phantom from afar?
Is it the hydrogen of the mire?
Would that its origin were higher!
Comes it not from a distant star?
Algol, or Vega of the Lyre? '

'That's for you to say, my boy! ' Mr. Nick nodded.
'That's your business! '

Lionel went on reading:

'To me, the soft and furtive breath
Of sylph, or elf, or sprite, it seems,
As lightly float its fitful gleams,
When slowly wakes the plain beneath
The morning's golden beams.

'Is it the glimmer of the lamp
Borne by the spectre, who would rest
On the roof-ridge where the wine is press'd,
When through the night-air chill and damp
The moon floats manifest?

'Is it the spirit of a fay,
That seeking, half concealed,
What peace a wicked world can yield,
Doth, like a gleaner, limp away,
Finding but nothing in the field? '

'Perfect! ' said Mr. Nick. 'Are you at the end of your
descriptive comparisons? '

'Oh! No, Mr. Nick,' said the clerk.

And he continued:

'Is it the image of a form
  That all acknowledge fair
  Distorted by the troubled air?
Or the last flash of the dying storm
  Traced by its lingering glare?

'Did it from the path escape,
  Traced by a falling meteorite
  That in its swift Icarian flight
Was luminous, had weight, and shape,
  And vanish'd in the night?

'Still on its path shoots radiance forth;
  And pale reflections cling,
  And rays of mystery fling,
Like the auroras of the north
  Light as a night-moth's wing!'

'What do you think of all this troubadourish jingle?'
Nick asked his fellow-passenger.

'I think,' the stranger replied, 'that your clerk has
imagination, and I'm curious to know what else he will
compare his will-o'-the-wisp to.'

'Go on then, Lionel.'

Lionel had blushed at the young man's compliment,
and with a clearer voice he read:

'Doth it glow in that hour of sighs
  When the living are a-bed,
  And the fluttering flag is spread,
That the Angel of the Darkness flies
  In the memory of the dead?'

'Brrr!' exclaimed Mr. Nick.

' When night is clothed in her gloomiest robe,
　　And the given time is nigh,
　　And hush'd is every cry,
　Is it the signal that the globe
　　Sends upwards to the sky?

' And such a light as on ocean floats
　　And, as the wandering spirits race
　　Along their weary voyage through space,
　The harbours of the universe denotes
　　And their lone resting-place? '

' Well done, young poet! ' the stranger complimented him.

' Yes, not bad! Not at all bad! ' said Mr. Nick. ' Where did you find all that, Lionel? That's all, I suppose? '

' No, Mr. Nick.' Lionel went on reading in a still more intense voice:

' But beware, dear maid, if in your eyes
　　The light of love it seems!
　　Chase it from your dreams!
　That light to flame will never rise
　　Brightly as it gleams! '

' A trap for the girls, indeed! ' said Mr. Nick. ' I should have been much surprised if there had not been a little love in view in these anacreontics! After all, it's the usual thing at your age! What do you think, sir? '

' Quite so,' said the stranger; ' and I fancy that . . .'

The stranger stopped in the middle of the sentence at the sight of a group of men at the side of the road, one of whom was hailing the driver to stop.

The horses were pulled up and the men approached the vehicle.

' Mr. Nick, I believe! ' said one of the men, lifting his hat.

' And Mr. Rip! ' and the lawyer added in an undertone: ' We must mind what we're up to! '

Luckily neither Mr. Nick, nor his clerk, nor the detective had noticed the change in the stranger's face when Rip's name was mentioned. He grew pale, with the paleness not of fear, but of that inspired by some unsurmountable horror. He would obviously have liked to hurl himself on the man. But, turning away his head, he managed to control himself.

' Are you off to Laval, Mr. Lawyer? ' asked Rip.

' As you see, Mr. Rip. Business will keep me there only an hour or two, and I hope to be back at Montreal this evening.'

' That's your business! '

' And what are you doing with your men? ' asked Mr. Nick. ' Always in ambush at the expense of the government. Are you going to capture some of those scoundrels? There are plenty of them, for they multiply like weeds. It would be much better for them to turn honest men . . .'

' That's so, but they haven't got the vocation for it.'

' The vocation! You're always joking, Mr. Rip! Are you on the track of some criminal? '

' Criminal to some; hero to others. It all depends on the point of view.'

' What do you mean? '

' The presence in the island has been reported of the famous Jean-Sans-Nom . . .'

' Ah! The famous Jean-Sans-Nom! Yes! The patriots have made him into a hero, and not without good reason! But her Gracious Majesty does not seem to be of the same opinion, or Gilbert Argall wouldn't have put you on his track.'

' That is so.'

' And you say they've seen this mysterious agitator in Montreal Island? '

' They say they've done so,' said Rip. ' But I'm beginning to doubt it.'

' Well, if he ever did come here, he's almost sure to have got away by this time,' Mr. Nick replied. ' He doesn't stay very long in one place. Jean-Sans-Nom won't be easy to get hold of.'

' Quite a will-o'-the-wisp,' the stranger smiled at the young clerk.

' Good! Very good! ' exclaimed Mr. Nick. ' Lionel, you ought to bow! And, by-the-bye, Mr. Rip, if you meet a will-o'-the-wisp on the road, will you please catch him by the collar, and bring him to my clerk? It will please the wandering flame to hear how he's been treated by a disciple of Apollo! '

' Certainly! ' said Rip. ' If we don't have to go back to Montreal, where I expect fresh instructions.'

Turning to the stranger, Rip continued:

' And you're accompanying Mr. Nick? '

' As far as Laval,' the stranger replied.

' Where I am in a hurry to go, too,' the lawyer added. ' Goodbye, Mr. Rip! If I can't wish you good luck, for the capture of Jean-Sans-Nom would be a sad blow for the patriots, I can at least wish you good morning! '

' And I can wish you good day, Mr. Nick.'

As the horses resumed their trot, Rip and his men vanished round a turning in the road.

A few minutes afterwards, the notary said to the stranger, who was leaning back in the corner:

'I do hope Jean-Sans-Nom won't let them catch him. They've been looking for him so long . . .'

'And they will have to go on looking!' exclaimed Lionel. 'And that damned Rip will lose his reputation . . .'

'Quiet, Lionel! That's none of our business.'

'This Jean-Sans-Nom seems used to outwitting the police!' put in the stranger.

'Just so, sir. If he's ever taken, it will be a great loss to the French-Canadians.'

'He won't lack comrades, Mr. Nick, and he isn't a man to let himself be taken.'

'It doesn't matter,' the lawyer replied. 'I've heard it would be a great pity. After all, I don't take so much interest in politics as Lionel, and it is better not to talk about them.'

'But,' continued the young man, 'we were interrupted when your clerk's poetical inspiration . . .'

'He's finished being inspired, I suppose?'

'No, Mr. Nick!' Lionel thanked the stranger with a smile.

'What, not out of breath yet?' exclaimed the notary. 'Here's a will-o'-the-wisp that was a sylph, an elf, a sprite, a spectre, a spirit, a phantom, a flash of lightning, a meteorite, a ray, a flag, a harbour-light, a spark of love, and I don't know what else! What else can it be?'

'I should like to know!' said the stranger.

'Then go on, Lionel, go on, and get to the end of it, if it has any end!'

Used to Mr. Nick's pleasantries, Lionel again began to read:

'Whate'er thou art, whate'er thy name,
 I would thy hidden projects know

And share thy very thoughts: and so,
Absorb'd in thee, mysterious flame,
    With thee would ever go.

' When settling on the silent trees
    Your wide wings in the twilight loom;
    Or, in the graveyard's darker gloom,
Softly call'd by the whispering breeze
    To guard the marble tomb.'

' Sad, sad! ' the lawyer murmured.

' Or where the seething billows race—
    The good ship driven on her side
    And by the tempest fiercely plied—
With all a spectre seagull's grace,
    About the labouring hull to glide.

' A closer union could we claim
    If fate would heed the prayer I lisp,
    To make us one, my will-o'-the-wisp!
To be born with you, my frolicsome flame!
    To die with you, my will-o'-the-wisp.'

' Ah! that's very good! ' said Mr. Nick. ' That's the
sort of ending that suits me. You might even sing it,'
and he hummed the last few words. ' What do you say,
sir? '

' Sir,' said the stranger. ' I hope the poet will accept
all my compliments; and maybe win the prize at the
meeting of the Lyre-Amicale. Whatever happens, his
verses have enabled me to pass a very pleasant time, and
never did a journey seem so short! '

Lionel was extremely flattered, and drank down the
stranger's praise. And Mr. Nick was not at all displeased
at the eulogiums addressed to his clerk.

Meanwhile the buggy had made good progress, and

eleven had just struck when they reached the northern branch of the river.

About this time the first steam-boats had already appeared on the St. Lawrence. They were not very powerful or very swift, and they resembled the modern 'tugs' more than anything else.

In a few minutes the boat took Mr. Nick, his clerk and their fellow-passenger across the middle branch of the river, whose greenish waters were still mingling with the blackish waters of the Ottawa.

There they parted company, after many compliments and much hand-shaking. Then, while the stranger walked straight into Laval, Mr. Nick and Lionel turned off away from the town, towards the east of the island.

CHAPTER IV

THE VILLA MONTCALM

J ESUS I SLAND, between the two upper arms of the St. Lawrence, includes the county of Laval. This is also the name of the island's chief town, situated on its northern bank. M. de Vaudreuil's house was three miles further down the St. Lawrence, and was built on its very edge, the lower step of its terrace being washed by the river.

M. de Vaudreuil had taken part in all the recent insurrections of the French-Canadians and had figured in the plot which the treason of Simon Morgaz had ended so tragically. A few years later an amnesty had restored him to freedom.

Here the manners were those of the seventeenth century. As an English author has very justly said, ' Lower Canada is a France of the olden time, under the white fleurdelisé flag,' and a French author points out that ' It is the field of refuge of the old régime. It is a Brittany or a Vendée of sixty years ago. On the American continent the colonist has treasured with jealous care the modes of thought, the naïve beliefs and the super- stitions of his fathers.' This was still true; the French race had stayed very pure in Canada, and without any admixture of foreign blood.

On returning to the Villa Montcalm, in 1829, M. de Vaudreuil found himself in easy circumstances. Although his fortune was not large, yet he could have stayed in retirement had not his over-ardent patriotism forced him into aggressive politics.

He was then forty-seven years of age; his greyish hair made him appear somewhat older; but his quick glance, his keen blue eyes, his tall stature, his robust constitution, which assured his health under all trials, and his sympathetic and prepossessing face, made him the perfect type of a French gentleman. He was a true descendant of the courageous noblemen who crossed the Atlantic in the eighteenth century to found the most beautiful of colonies, which the odious carelessness of Louis XIV had abandoned to Great Britain.

He had been a widower for ten years. The death of the wife he had loved with the deepest affection had left an irreparable void in his existence. His life was now centred in his only daughter, in whom her mother lived again.

Clary de Vaudreuil was then in her twentieth year. Her graceful figure, her abundant dark brown hair, her large glowing eyes, her rich colour, and her somewhat serious expression, made her like some of Fennimore Cooper's heroines, handsome rather than pretty, and commanding rather than attractive. As a rule, she maintained a rigid reserve, or rather her whole life was concentrated in the only love she had yet felt—the love of her country.

Clary de Vaudreuil was a patriot. During the events of 1832 and 1834, she had closely studied the various phases of the insurrection. The leaders of the opposition regarded her as the bravest of the many women whose devotion they had secured. And when M. de Vaudreuil's political friends met at the Villa, Clary took part in their discussions, saying little, but listening, observing, and entering into correspondence with the local committees.

The French had absolute confidence in her, for she deserved it; they had the most respectful friendship for her, and she was worthy of it.

However, in her impassioned heart another love had come of late to mingle with her love for her country—a love ideal and vague, which did not even know him by whom it was inspired.

In 1831 and 1834, a mysterious personage had played an important part in the many attempts at rebellion. He had risked his head with an audacity, a courage, a disinterestedness, that were well calculated to impress the imagination of the sensitive. Throughout Lower Canada his name was repeated with enthusiasm—or rather the formula that served him for a name, which was none other than Jean-Sans-Nom. In the day of battle he came to the, very forefront; when the strife was over, he disappeared. But it was felt that he was acting in the dark, that his hand never ceased to prepare for the future. In vain the authorities had sought to discover his hiding-place. Even Rip and Co. had failed. Nothing was known of the man's origin, of his past or present life. One thing only was certain, that his influence was all-powerful among the French-Canadians. And a legend had risen around him, and the reformists waited to see him appear, waving the flag of independence.

Such was the anonymous hero whose deeds had made so deep an impression on Clary de Vaudreuil. Her most secret thoughts invariably turned to him. She regarded him as a supernatural being. She lived in mystic communion with him. In loving Jean-Sans-Nom with the most ideal of loves, it seemed to her she loved her country all the more. But this sentiment she kept close in her heart. And when her father saw her wandering away in the park, and moving so pensively, he little realised that she was dreaming of the young patriot who in her eyes symbolised the revolution.

Among the political friends who often met at the Villa Montcalm, there were many whose relatives had taken part with M. de Vaudreuil in the ill-fated conspiracy of 1825. Among these friends were Andrew Farran and William Clerc, whose brothers Robert and Francis had been executed on 28th September; as well as Vincent Hodge, the son of Walter Hodge, who had been betrayed with his comrades by Simon Morgaz. With them a Quebec lawyer, the Deputy Sebastian Gramont—in whose house it had been falsely reported to Rip that Jean-Sans-Nom had been a visitor—often shared in the hospitality of M. de Vaudreuil.

The most ardent of these was certainly Vincent Hodge, then a young man of thirty-two. Of American descent by his father, he was of French descent by his mother, who had died of grief a short time after her husband's execution. Vincent Hodge had found it impossible to live near Clary, without admiring her, without loving her; nor was this in any way displeasing to M. de Vaudreuil. Vincent Hodge was a distinguished-looking man, genial and pleasant in manner, though a little too much of the typical frontier Yankee. Clary could not have chosen a husband more worthy of her—brave beyond reproach, earnest in character, and true in feeling; but she had not even noticed that she was the object of his attention. Between her and Vincent Hodge there could be only one bond—that of patriotism. She realised his good qualities, but she could not love him. Her life, her thoughts, her aspirations, belonged to another, to an unknown stranger for whom she was waiting, and who would one day appear.

M. de Vaudreuil and his friends watched attentively the progress of events in the Canadian provinces. Opinion was in a very excited state, but it no longer restricted itself, as in 1825, to a mere personal plot against the Governor. It was rather a general conspiracy in a state of latent heat. For the rebellion to break out it only needed a leader to appeal to the people, and to raise every parish in the adjoining country. And then, without a doubt, M. de Vaudreuil and his friends would take a leading part in the insurrection.

Never had circumstances been more favourable. The Reformists were loud in their protests, denouncing the exactions of the Government which claimed that it was empowered by the British Cabinet to seize on the public revenue without the consent of the legislature. The newspapers—among them the *Canadian* founded in 1806, and the *Vindicator* of more recent origin—fulminated against the Crown and its agents. They reported the speeches made in Parliament or in public meetings by Papineau and many others who rivalled each other in the talent and audacity of their attacks. A spark would be enough to provoke a popular explosion. This was well known to Lord Gosford, and the supporters of the French were as fully aware of this as his lordship.

Such was the position when, on the morning of 3rd September, a letter arrived at the Villa Montcalm. Posted the night before at Montreal, it informed M. de Vaudreuil that his friends, Vincent Hodge, Andrew Farran, and William Clerc had been invited to visit him that evening. M. de Vaudreuil did not recognise the hand which had written the letter, whose only signature was: A Son of Freedom.

M. de Vaudreuil was much surprised at the communication, and also at the way in which it had been made. The night before he had seen his friends at Montreal, at the house of one of them, and had left them without anything being said of a meeting on the morrow. Had the others received a similar letter? That might be so; but might it not be some plot on the part of the police? This suspicion was natural enough after the Simon Morgaz experience.

But all that could be done was to wait. When Vincent Hodge, Farran and Clerc arrived—if they did arrive—they could perhaps explain what at present seemed inexplicable. Such was Clary's opinion when she read the letter. Her eyes were riveted on the mysterious writing as she examined it attentively. A strange spirit was here. Where her father saw only a snare spread for himself and his political friends, she seemed, on the contrary, to believe in some powerful intervention on behalf of the French cause. Was there at last to be revealed the hand that would seize the threads of a new uprising, and guide it to success?

' Father,' she said, ' I can trust him! '

However, as the rendezvous was appointed for the evening, M. de Vaudreuil thought he would first go over to Leval, where he might learn what had happened to render it necessary. He could be there to receive Vincent Hodge and his two friends when they landed on the island. But just as he was going to give the order to get ready, his servant appeared to inform him that a visitor had arrived.

' Who is he? ' M. de Vaudreuil asked quickly.

' Here is his card,' said the servant.

M. de Vaudreuil took the card, read the name it bore, and immediately exclaimed:

' The excellent Mr. Nick? He's always welcome, ask him in! '

And the lawyer found himself in the presence of M. de Vaudreuil and his daughter.

' You, Mr. Nick! ' exclaimed M. de Vaudreuil.

' In person, and ready to pay my respects to yourself and to Mademoiselle Clary! '

And he shook hands with M. de Vaudreuil, after having favoured his daughter with the official salute which the older lawyers have reserved for themselves from time immemorial.

' Mr. Nick,' said M. de Vaudreuil, ' this is an unexpected visit, but it is a pleasant one nevertheless.'

' Very pleasant for me,' replied Mr. Nick. ' And how are you, Monsieur de Vaudreuil? You both look quite well. You certainly seem to live well at the Villa Montcalm! I ought to take back to Bon Secours a little of the air you breathe here.'

' You needn't do that, Mr. Nick! Come and see us oftener.'

' And stay a few days,' Clary added.

' And my office, and my deeds! ' exclaimed the loquacious notary. ' They won't leave me much time for holiday-making! To say nothing of the wills, for people live to be so old in Canada that they'll end by never dying. What with our octogenarians and centenarians, we are a long way out of the bounds of ordinary statistics. But as for marriage settlements, they completely tire me out! By-the-bye, six weeks ago I was at Laprairie with one of my clients—one of my good clients, you understand—when I had to draw up the settlements for his nineteenth youngster! '

'That must be my farmer Thomas Harcher, I'll wager! ' exclaimed M. de Vaudreuil.

'Exactly, and it was to your farm at Chipogan that I went.'

'That's a large family, Mr. Nick.'

'It is that, Monsieur de Vaudreuil, and note that I'm in no hurry to get quit of the documents that concern it.'

'Well, Mr. Nick,' said Clary, ' we're likely to meet you at Chipogan. Thomas Harcher has so warmly insisted on our being present at his daughter's wedding, that, if nothing keeps us here, my father and I are going to give him that pleasure! '

'And give me that pleasure too,' said Mr. Nick. ' Isn't it a pleasure for me to see you! I have only one complaint to make, Mademoiselle Clary.'

'And what is that Mr. Nick? '

'That you always receive me here as a friend and never as a lawyer.'

Clary smiled at the insinuation, and almost immediately resumed her habitual gravity.

'But,' said M. de Vaudreuil, ' it is not as a friend, my dear Nick, that you are here today—you've come as a lawyer! '

'So I have! So I have! But not on account of Mademoiselle Clary! But all in good time! The time will come right enough! But, Monsieur de Vaudreuil, I beg to inform you that I have not come alone.'

'What! You have a companion? And you let him wait in the antechamber? I'll invite him in.'

'No! No! It isn't worth while! It's only my clerk—

C

a boy who makes verses—did you ever hear of such a
thing?—and who runs after will-o'-the-wisps. Imagine a
clerk-poet, or a poet-clerk, Mademoiselle Clary! As I
wanted to speak with you in private, M. de Vaudreuil, I
told him to take a walk in the park.'

' You were quite right, Mr. Nick! But we must refresh
this young poet.'

' Useless! He drinks nothing but nectar, and not even
that unless it's of the latest vintage.'

M. de Vaudreuil could not help laughing at the jokes of
this excellent man, whom he had known for so many
years, and whose advice had always proved so valuable
in the management of his personal affairs.

' I'll leave you with my father, Mr. Nick,' said Clary.

' I beg that you'll stay, mademoiselle! ' replied the
lawyer. ' I know I can speak in your presence, even of
things that may have reference to politics—at least I
suppose so, for as you know, I never meddle . . .'

' Well, well, Mr. Nick,' M. de Vaudreuil agreed. ' Clary
can be present at our interview. Sit down, and then you
can talk at your ease.'

The lawyer took one of the cane chairs while M. de
Vaudreuil and his daughter settled down on a sofa in
front of him.

' And now, my dear Nick,' began M. de Vaudreuil,
' what has brought you here? '

' To give you this,' said the notary.

And he drew from his pocket a bundle of bank-notes.

' Money! ' M. de Vaudreuil could not hide his extreme
surprise.

' Yes, money, and good money, and, whether it pleases
you or not, a good round sum! '

' A good round sum! '

' Judge for yourself! Fifty thousand dollars in beautiful notes of legal currency.'

' And this money is intended . . .'

' For you—for you alone! '

' And who sent it me? '

' Impossible for me to tell you, for the very excellent reason that I don't know! '

' What use is to be made of this money? '

' Neither do I know that.'

' And how have you been instructed to remit me such a sum? '

' Read! '

The notary handed him a letter containing only a few lines:

' Mr. Nick, lawyer at Montreal, will at once remit to the president of the Reformist Committee of Laval at the Villa Montcalm, the balance standing to our account in his office books.

' J. B. J.

' September 2nd, 1837.'

M. de Vaudreuil looked at the lawyer, understanding as little as ever the reason for his errand.

' Mr. Nick,' he asked, ' where was this letter posted? '

' At Saint Charles, in the county of Verchères.'

Clary took the letter. She examined the writing. Perhaps it was in the same hand as the letter which notified M. de Vaudreuil of the impending visit of his friends? No! Nothing of the sort. There was no resemblance between the handwriting of the two letters, as she pointed out to her father.

' You have no suspicion, Mr. Nick,' she asked, ' who the writer of this letter is, the man who signs himself J. B. J.? '

' None, Mademoiselle Clary.'

' But it isn't the first time you've been in touch with this person? '

' Evidently.'

' Or rather with these persons, for the letter does not say my account, but our account, which would lead us to think that the three initials belong to three different names.'

' Quite so,' said Mr. Nick.

' I notice too,' said M. de Vaudreuil, that, as it's a question of a balance, you must have made certain payments before this.'

' Monsieur de Vaudreuil,' the lawyer began. ' I'll tell you all I know, and what I think you ought to know! '

And, taking time to collect his thoughts, he continued :

' In 1825, a month after the sentence which cost the lives of some of your dearest friends, and deprived you of your liberty, I received a packet containing bank-notes amounting to the enormous sum of one hundred thousand dollars. The packet had been posted at Quebec, and contained a letter which read : ' This sum of one hundred thousand dollars is placed in the hands of Mr. Nick, lawyer, of Montreal, for him to dispose of, according to instructions which he will receive later. His discretion is counted on to say nothing of the deposit entrusted to his care, nor of the use to which it may eventually be put '.'

' And it was signed? ' asked Clary.

' It was signed J. B. J.,' answered Mr. Nick.

' The same initials? ' said M. de Vaudreuil.

' The same? ' repeated Clary.

' Yes, mademoiselle. As you may think, I could not be more surprised than I was at this mysterious deposit. But after all, as I could not send back the money to my unknown client, and as I did not care to inform the authorities, I paid in the hundred thousand dollars to the bank at Montreal, and I waited.'

Clary de Vaudreuil and her father listened to Mr. Nick with the greatest attention. Had not the lawyer said that in his opinion the money was intended for political purposes? And, as they were soon to see, he was not deceived.

' Six years later,' he continued, ' a sum of twenty-two thousand dollars was asked for in a letter signed with these enigmatic initials, to be sent to the village of Berthier.'

' To whom? ' asked M. de Vaudreuil.

' To the chairman of the Reformist Committee—and a little later there broke out the revolt you remember. Four years elapsed, and, in a letter signed with the same initials, I was requested to send twenty-eight thousand dollars to Sainte Martine, this time to the president of the Chateauguay Committee. A month later there came that violent reaction which marked the election of 1834, and brought about the prorogation of the House, followed by the demand to impeach the Governor Lord Aylmer! '

M. de Vaudreuil reflected a few moments on this; then he said:

' And so, my dear Nick, you can see a connection between these different demonstrations, and the despatch of the money to the reformist committees.'

' I, Monsieur de Vaudreuil! ' Mr. Nick protested. ' I can see nothing! I am not a politician! I am a simple administrator! I have only to return the sums I have received on deposit, and in the way I am instructed. I tell you just what happened and I leave you to draw your own conclusions.'

' Good! My prudent friend! ' M. de Vaudreuil smiled. ' We will not compromise you. But if you have come today to the Villa Montcalm . . .'

' It is to do for the third time what I have already done twice. This morning, the third of September, I have been instructed, first, to dispose of the balance of the sum that had been remitted to me, being fifty thousand dollars; and, secondly, to place it in the hands of the president of the Committee at Laval. That is why, M. de Vaudreuil, you being the president of the said Committee, I have brought you the said sum. Now, to what use is it to be put? I do not know, and I do not want to know. It is in the hands of the president mentioned in the letter, and if I did not send it through the post, but preferred to bring it myself, it was because it gave me an opportunity of seeing my friend, Monsieur de Vaudreuil and his daughter Mademoiselle Clary! '

Mr. Nick had finished his story without interruption. And then, having said what he wanted to say, he arose, went out on to the terrace, and looked at the boats going up and down the river.

M. de Vaudreuil, deep in his reflections, kept silence. A similar train of thought was exercising the mind of his daughter. He had no doubt that this money, mysteriously deposited with Mr. Nick, was to be employed for the needs of the cause, and for an approaching insurrection. Was it not a singular coincidence that the money had come the very day that ' A Son of Freedom ' had called together the most intimate friends of M. de Vaudreuil?

The conversation was resumed, and continued for some time. And with the loquacious Mr. Nick how could it be otherwise? He informed M. de Vaudreuil of what M. de Vaudreuil knew far better, the political situation in Lower Canada. And these things, as he did not cease to repeat, he only spoke of with extreme reserve, protesting that he had no desire to be mixed up in them. His object was to put M. de Vaudreuil on his guard, for there had certainly been an increase in the activity of the police around Montreal. Then he added:

'What the authorities particularly dread is that a leader should put himself at the head of a popular movement, and that this leader should be the famous Jean-Sans-Nom.'

At these words Clary rose, and went to lean on the window-sill overlooking the park.

'Do you then know this daring agitator?' asked M. de Vaudreuil.

'I do not know him,' replied the lawyer. 'I have never seen him, and I never met anybody who did know him. But he exists, there's not a doubt about that! And I imagine him as a true hero of romance—a young man of tall stature, of noble features, and a stirring voice—unless he is some good old patriarch, bent and broken by age. With such people you don't know what to think!'

'Whatever he may be,' M. de Vaudreuil replied, 'Heaven grant that he may think of putting himself at our head; then we'll follow him as far as he likes to lead us.'

'Well, Monsieur de Vaudreuil, that may not be long in happening.'

'You're trying to tell us?' Clary returned at once to the middle of the room.

'I say, Mademoiselle Clary—or rather, I say nothing! That's wiser!'

'Speak! speak!' the girl implored him. 'What do you know?'

' What others no doubt know,' replied Mr. Nick. ' That Jean-Sans-Nom has reappeared near Montreal. At least, so runs the rumour—unfortunately—'

' Unfortunately? ' asked Clary.

' Yes, for if so, I fear our hero won't be able to escape the police. This very day as I was crossing the island of Montreal I met the bloodhounds that Gilbert Argall had put on his track, and among them was the head of the house of Rip and Co.'

' What? Rip? ' said M. de Vaudreuil.

' Himself,' replied the lawyer. ' He's a clever man, and he can be stimulated by a good reward. If he catches Jean-Sans-Nom, the condemnation of the young patriot —yes, he certainly ought to be young—his condemnation is certain, and the national party will have provided another victim.'

In spite of her self-control, Clary turned pale, her eyes closed, and it was with difficulty she could restrain the beatings of her heart. M. de Vaudreuil walked hurriedly up and down about the room.

Mr. Nick, anxious to remove the painful effect of his last words, added :

' After all, he's a man of uncommon audacity, this Jean-Sans-Nom. Up to the present, he's managed to escape. And if he's closely pressed, every house in the county will give him a refuge, and all doors will be open to him—even the door of Mr. Nick's office, although Mr. Nick does not meddle with politics.'

Thereupon the lawyer took his leave of M. and Mademoiselle de Vaudreuil. He had no time to spare if he wished to return to Montreal before dinner-time— that regular and ever-welcome hour at which he completed one of the most important deeds of his existence.

M. de Vaudreuil would have had the horses brought out to give him a lift to Laval; but, like a prudent man, Mr. Nick declined. The less that was known of his visit to the villa Montcalm the better. He had good legs, thank Heaven, and a mile or more less would not trouble one of the best walkers among the lawyers of Canada. And was he not of the blood of the Sagamores, the descendant of those hardy Indian people whose warriors for months used to follow the war-path, and so on.

In short, Mr. Nick called Lionel, who no doubt had been following the muses along the paths of the park; and, a little up-stream, they soon reached the road to Laval.

In three-quarters of an hour they reached the quay just as Vincent Hodge, Clerc and Farran were landing from the tug on their way to the Villa Montcalm.

As they passed, the lawyer was saluted with the inevitable ' Good morning, Mr. Nick! ' Crossing the river, he and his clerk got into the buggy, and they returned to the house on Bon Secours market-place just as the old servant Dolly was placing the soup on the table.

Mr. Nick at once sat down in his large arm-chair, and as Lionel took his place opposite he could hear him humming:

' To be born with you, my frolicsome flame,

To die with you, my will-o'-the-wisp.

' And above all,' he added, ' if you swallow a few verses when you eat, please look out for the bones.'*

*This may be one of the puns to which Verne was addicted, the French word *vers* meaning either ' verses ' or ' worms! '—I.O.E.

CHAPTER V

THE STRANGER

W H E N V I N C E N T H O D G E, William Clerc and Andrew Farran reached the villa, they were welcomed by M. de Vaudreuil.

Clary had just gone to her room. By the window opening on to the park she let her looks wander over the countryside. The thought of this mysterious being, so vividly recalled to her memory, filled her whole mind. He had been reported in the district. He was being hunted for near Montreal. For this island to offer him a refuge he would only have to cross an arm of the river! Would he seek shelter at the Villa Montcalm? That friends were there ready to welcome him he could not doubt. But to take shelter under the roof of M. de Vaudreuil, the president of one of the Reformist Committees, would expose him to the greatest danger. Would not the villa be specially watched? Yet Clary had a presentiment that Jean-Sans-Nom would come, were it only for a day, an hour. And in her exalted state, anxious to be alone, she had left the drawing-room before M. de Vaudreuil's friends were introduced.

William Clerc and Andrew Farran—both about the same age as M. de Vaudreuil—were two ex-officers of the Canadian militia. Deprived of their rank after the sentence which had sent their brothers to the scaffold, and themselves condemned to imprisonment for life, they had regained their liberty only through the amnesty to which M. de Vaudreuil owed his. The party saw in them two men of action who only sought another opportunity of risking their lives in an appeal to arms. They were energetic, and inured to fatigue by their experience as hunters on their own estates.

As soon as Vincent Hodge had grasped M. de Vaudreuil's hand, he asked him whether he knew that he and the others had been personally invited by letter?

'Yes,' replied M. de Vaudreuil; 'and no doubt the letter you received, like my own, was signed " A Son of Freedom "?'

'That is so,' Farran agreed.

'You don't suspect an ambush?' asked Clerc. 'In arranging this rendezvous, mayn't they mean to catch us when we're all together?'

'The Legislative Council,' M. de Vaudreuil reminded him, 'has not yet deprived Canadians of the right of visiting one another's homes—at least as far as I know!'

'Perhaps not,' Farran demurred, 'but who sent that letter, and why didn't he sign his name?'

'That's certainly strange,' M. de Vaudreuil replied, 'especially as this person, whoever he may be, doesn't say that he'll be present at the rendezvous. The letter I had merely informed me that you three were to meet me here this evening . . .'

'And ours said no more,' put in Clerc.

'It's difficult to understand,' Vincent Hodge commented, 'why this mysterious person should have arranged matters like this if he didn't mean to be present; and I believe he'll come.'

'Well!' replied Farran; 'let him come. We shall see what sort of a man he is, and we'll listen to what he has to say. And if it doesn't suit us to have anything to do with him, we can soon show him out.'

' Vaudreuil? ' asked Clerc. ' Your daughter knows about this letter, what does she think? '

' She doesn't feel suspicious,' M. de Vaudreuil assured them.

' We must wait,' said Vincent Hodge.

But if he intended to be at the rendezvous, the man who signed the letter would have to take some precautions. It would be night before he reached the villa—at least in the circumstnaces that would only be prudent.

Conversation ranged over the political situation, now so critical because of the repressive meastres of the English parliament. Such a state of things could not last. And in this connection, M. de Vaudreuil added that, as president of Laval Committee, he had received from Mr. Nick, the lawyer, a considerable sum which was certainly intended for the use of the cause.

As they walked in the park until dinner was ready, Vincent Hodge, Clerc and Farran confirmed what Mr. Nick had said. The police were on the alert. Not only were Rip and his men in action, but detachments of regular police were also scouring the country, doing their utmost to get on the trail of Jean-Sans-Nom. His appearance would obviously be enough to provoke a rising. So it was not impossible that the stranger was to let M. de Vaudreuil know about this.

Towards six, M. de Vaudreuil and his friends returned to the drawing-room, where they found Clary. William Clerc and Farran greeted her in the paternal way authorised by their age and their long friendship. Vincent Hodge was more reserved. Respectfully he shook hands, then he offered her his arm, and led the way into the dining-room.

The dinner was abundant, as was then usual in Canada in the humblest as well as in the richest houses. It consisted of fish from the river, venison from the neighbouring forests, and vegetables and fruits gathered in the villa's kitchen-garden.

During the meal, nothing was said about the meeting so impatiently awaited. Before the servants it was best to say nothing, although they had been in the family service for years.

After dinner, the evening was so fine, the temperature so mild, that Clary went and sat under the verandah. The St. Lawrence caressed the lower steps of the terrace, bathing them with its waters in the twilight. M. de Vaudreuil and his guests smoked as they walked beside the balustrades, exchanging only a few words, and these in a low voice.

It was just after seven. Night began to close in and hide the lower depths of the valleys, while the long twilight withdrew across the western plains; the stars began to appear in opposite part of the sky.

Clary looked up and down the St. Lawrence. Would the stranger come by water? This seemed likely, if he wished to leave no trace of his passage. It was easy for a small boat to slip along the river among the grass and reeds of its bank. If he landed at the terrace, he could enter the villa without being seen, and could leave it again without the rest of the people in the house having the slightest suspicion of his presence.

As, however, it was possible that the visitor might not come by the St. Lawrence, M. de Vaudreuil had given orders to admit at once anyone who called at the villa.

A lamp in the drawing-room showed only a gleam of light through the curtains of the windows, which were moreover sheltered by the thick glass of the verandah. From outside nothing could be seen of what was happening indoors.

But if all was quiet on the park side, things were very different along the river. Boats occasionally came into view, sometimes making for the left bank, sometimes for the right; they might meet, then a few words were exchanged, and they rowed away in different directions.

M. de Vaudreuil and his friends carefully watched these comings and goings, whose object they fully realised.

'Those are police boats,' said Clerc.

'Yes,' agreed Vincent Hodge, 'and they're watching the river—and . . .'

'Perhaps the Villa Montcalm! '

The words were spoken in a low voice, and it was neither M. de Vaudreuil nor his daughter, nor either of his guests, who had uttered them.

A man, formerly hidden among the thick grass below the balustrade, appeared on the right of the steps, and hurriedly crossed the terrace. He raised his cap, made a slight bow, and said:

'The Son of Freedom who wrote to you, gentlemen! '

M. de Vaudreuil and the others, amazed at his sudden appearance, tried to recognise the man who had entered the villa in so unceremonious a fashion. His voice was as unknown to them as his face.

'Monsieur de Vaudreuil,' the newcomer explained, 'you must excuse my coming here like this, but it was essential that nobody should see me come, just as it is that nobody should see me go.'

'Come in,' M. de Vaudreuil invited him.

They all entered the drawing-room, and the door was closed.

The man was the young stranger in whose company Mr. Nick had travelled from Montreal, and M. de Vaudreuil and his friends realised, as the lawyer had done, that he was a French Canadian.

After bidding adieu to Mr. Nick at Laval he had gone to a humble tavern in the lower part of the town. There, in a dark corner of the room, he had waited till dinner time, glancing through the newspapers. His impassive countenance gave no sign of the feelings aroused by what he read, although the journals were most violent in taking sides for or against the Crown. Queen Victoria had just succeeded to her uncle, William the Fourth, and in impassioned articles a discussion was being carried on as to the changes which the new reign would bring about in Canada. But although it was a woman's hand that held the sceptre of the United Kingdom, it was feared that it would rest heavily on the colony.

Till six the young man had stayed in the tavern where he dined, and at eight he had set out.

If a spy had followed him, he would have seen him make for the river bank, creep through the thick grass, and reach the villa, where he arrived three-quarters of an hour later. There the stranger had waited awhile before appearing on the terrace, and had interrupted the conversation between M. de Vaudreuil and his friends.

And now, with the doors and windows shut, they could speak without fear of being overheard.

'Sir,' M. de Vaudreuil began, 'you will not be surprised if I first ask you who you are?'

' I told you when I arrived, M. de Vaudreuil. I am, like all of you, a Son of Freedom.'

Clary made an involuntary gesture of disappointment. Perhaps she had expected another name than this, so widespread among the French-Canadian agitators. Would this man persist in keeping to his incognito even in the Villa Montcalm?

' Sir,' Farran addressed him, ' if you arranged a meeting here between us and Monsieur de Vaudreuil, it was no doubt to confer with us on matters of some importance. Before talking freely to you, it is only natural that we should like to know whom we are dealing with.'

' You would have been imprudent, gentlemen, not to have asked me that question,' the young man replied. ' And it would be unpardonable of me if I refused to answer it.'

And he handed them a letter.

The letter informed M. de Vaudreuil of the visit of the stranger, in whom, it assured him, he might place entire confidence, even if he did not give his name. It was signed by one of the principal leaders of the Opposition in Parliament, the lawyer Gramont, deputy for Quebec, and one of the political associates of M. de Vaudreuil. Gramont added that if the visitor asked the latter for hospitality over a few days, he could be granted this with every confidence that it was in the interest of the cause.

M. de Vaudreuil read this letter to the others, and replied:

' Sir, you can consider yourself at home here, and you can stay as long as it suits you at the Villa Montcalm.'

' Two days at the outside, Monsieur de Vaudreuil,' the young man assured him. ' In four days I must rejoin my companions at the mouth of the St. Lawrence. I thank you for your welcome. And now, gentlemen, I beg you to listen to what I have to say.'

He then described in detail the state of public opinion at the moment, and explained that the country was ready to rise against the loyalists and the agents of the Crown. This he had seen for himself in a Reformist campaign held during the last few weeks along the Upper St. Lawrence and the Ottawa. In a few days he was to pay a last visit to the parishes in the eastern counties, so as to knit together the elements of an approaching insurrection, which would extend from the mouth of the river as far as Ontario. To this levy in mass neither Lord Gosford, with the representatives of authority, nor General Colborne, with a few thousand redcoats, had sufficient forces to oppose, and Canada—he had no doubt—would at last throw off the oppressor's yoke.

' A province torn from its homeland,' he ended, ' is like a child torn from her mother. It ought to be claimed without respite, fought for without mercy. It should never be forgotten.'

The stranger spoke with a coolness that showed that always and everywhere he could retain his self-control; that a fire burned within him; and that his thoughts were inspired by the most ardent patriotism. As he gave certain details as to what he had done and what he meant to do, Clary never took her eyes off him. Everything he said told her that she had before her the hero in whom, in her imagination, the Canadian revolution was incarnate.

When he had finished explaining his plans, he added:

' A leader is needed by those who claim our autonomy, and when the time comes a leader will arise to take the lead. Meanwhile a committee of action should be formed to correlate the individual efforts. Will you and your friends join this committee? All of you have already suffered in your families, in your persons, for the national cause. This cause has cost the lives of our best patriots, of your father, Vincent Hodge, of your brothers, William Clerc and Andrew Farran . . .'

' By the treason of a scoundrel! ' said Vincent Hodge.

' Yes, of a scoundrel! ' repeated the young man. And Clary detected a slight change in his voice, hitherto so clear. ' But,' he added, ' the man is dead.'

' Are you sure of that? ' asked Clerc.

' He is dead,' the stranger was quite definite, though it was hard to see how he could possibly know.

' Dead! This Simon Morgaz! And it was not I who did justice on him! ' exclaimed Vincent Hodge.

' My friends,' said M. de Vaudreuil, ' let us say no more about the traitor, and allow me to reply to the suggestion we have just heard. Sir,' he turned to his guest, ' what our comrades have already done we are prepared to do. We will risk our lives as they risked theirs. You can depend on us unreservedly, and we will undertake to centralise at this Villa Montcalm all the efforts in which you have taken the initiative. We are in every-day touch with the various committees in the district, and at the first signal we shall be ready. You mean, you say, to leave us in two days to visit the eastern parishes? Be it so. At your return you will find us ready to follow the leader, whoever he may be, who will unfurl the flag of independence.'

' Vaudreuil has spoken for us all,' agreed Vincent Hodge. ' We have but one thought—to release our country from oppression and to ensure her freedom.'

' And which, this time, she shall conquer! ' Clary

moved towards the young man. But just then he was going towards the door that opened on to the terrace.

'Listen, gentlemen!' he told them.

A vague sound could be heard in the direction of Laval; a distant clamour, whose nature and purpose it was difficult to recognise.

'What is that?' asked William Clerc.

'Has the rising begun already?' asked Farran.

'Heaven grant it may not!' Clary murmured. 'It would be premature.'

'Yes, premature,' the stranger agreed.

'What can it be?' asked M. de Vaudreuil. 'Listen! The noise is coming nearer.'

'It sounds like a trumpet-call,' Farran pointed out.

Brazen notes resounding through space at regular intervals could be heard at the villa. Was it an armed detachment making for M. de Vaudreuil's house?

M. de Vaudreuil opened the door of the room, and his friends followed him out on the terrace.

They stared towards the west, but there was no suspicious-looking light in that direction; the sound was obviously not coming across the island. But suddenly a confused din was heard nearer, and at the same time there came a sound of trumpets.

'There it is,' Vincent Hodge pointed up-stream towards Laval. In that direction some torches were giving a light very little stronger than that reflected by the misty waters of the river.

Two or three minutes passed. A boat dropping down with the tide approached the bank a quarter of a mile up-stream. It contained a dozen men, whose uniform it was easy to recognise in the torchlight. It was a detachment of the police.

From time to time the boat stopped, and then a voice, preceded by a blast from the trumpet, resounded through the air. But at the Villa Montcalm they could not hear what it was saying.

' That's a proclamation,' William Clerc suggested.

' And it ought to be something important,' Farran responded, ' for the authorities to issue it at this hour.'

' Wait,' M. de Vaudreuil told them, ' and we'll soon hear ....'

' Wouldn't it be safer for us to go back into the drawing-room? ' Clary asked the stranger.

' Why should we? ' he replied. ' What the authorities think good enough to proclaim ought to be good enough for us to hear.'

Meanwhile, the boat, rowed downstream and followed by a few canoes, had come opposite the terrace.

A blast was given by the trumpet, then some words rang out quite clearly:

' BY THE GOVERNOR-GENERAL OF THE
CANADIAN PROVINCES
' A Proclamation
This 3rd of September, 1837.

' A reward is hereby offered for Jean-Sans-Nom, who has reappeared in the counties of the Upper St. Lawrence. Six thousand dollars will be paid to whoever will arrest him, or who gives information leading to his arrest.

' For Lord Gosford,
' Gilbert Argall,
' Minister for Police.'

Then the boat continued on its course down stream.

M. de Vaudreuil and his friends stayed motionless on the terrace, which was then shrouded by the darkness of the night. Not a movement had the stranger made as the constable's voice repeated the terms of the proclamation. But the girl, though almost unconsciously, had taken a step towards him.

M. de Vaudreuil was the first to speak.

' Again a reward offered to traitors! ' he said. ' It will be useless this time, I hope, for the good name of the Canadian loyalists! '

' It's too much for them to hope they'll find another Simon Morgaz! ' exclaimed Vincent Hodge.

' May God protect Jean-Sans-Nom! ' Clary's voice trembled with emotion.

There were a few moments' silence.

' Let's come in and go to our rooms,' M. de Vaudreuil suggested. ' I'll see that one is got ready for you,' he added, turning to the stranger.

' Thank you,' was the reply; ' but it is impossible for me to stay any longer in this house . . .'

' But why? '

' When, an hour ago, I accepted the hospitality you offered me, I was not in the position where this proclamation has put me.'

' What do you mean? '

' That my presence can now only compromise you, for the Governor-General has put a price on my head. I am Jean-Sans-Nom! '

And Jean-Sans-Nom bowed, and was walking towards the river bank, when Clary held him back.

' Stay here,' she said.

CHAPTER VI

THE ST. LAWRENCE

The valley of the St. Lawrence is probably one of the largest in the world, and traverses much of Lower Canada. But it is not till the middle of April that the ice accumulated during the long rigorous Canadian winter begins to break up. The river then becomes navigable, so that large vessels can reach the Great Lakes, those fresh-water seas which stretch, like a string of beads, across what has been so poetically called ' the Fenimore Cooper Country.' Then the river, served by the tide, is as lively as a roadstead when a peace treaty has just raised the blockade. Sailing-vessels, steamers, timber-rafts, pilot-boats, coasters, fishing-boats, pleasure-boats, and canoes glide on the surface of its waters, now clear of their icy covering. After half a year of death, it is half a year of life.

On 13th September, about six in the morning, a cutter left the little port of St. Anne, situated at the mouth of the St. Lawrence, on the southern bank. She was manned by five of those fishermen who sell their catch from village to village, or rather from house to house—for there is almost an unbroken series of houses along both banks.

This cutter carried a passenger who was a fisherman only in his dress. But it would have been difficult to recognise in him the young man who for two days had been a guest at the Villa Montcalm.

It was Jean-Sans-Nom.

While staying at the villa he had given no explanation of the incognito under which he concealed himself and his family. Jean—that was the only name he had given M. and Mademoiselle de Vaudreuil.

In the evening of 3rd September, when their conference was over, the other guests had returned to Montreal, but it was not till two days later that Jean took his leave.

During his short stay, what hours were passed in discussing the new attempt which was to free Canada from the English yoke! With what passion Clary heard the young patriot glorify the cause so dear to both of them! He seemed to have shaken off some of the coldness he had shown at first, and which seemed to be assumed. Perhaps he was responding to the influence of the spirit of the girl whose patriotism harmonised so well with his own.

It was on the evening of 5th September that Jean had left the villa to continue his wandering life, and to complete his reformist propaganda in Lower Canada. Nobody else in the house had suspected that he was Jean-Sans-Nom, nor had Rip and Co., diverted to a false trail, discovered his hiding-place. He had left the villa as secretly as he had reached it, crossed the St. Lawrence, and struck into the interior, towards the American frontier, so as to be able to cross it if necessary. As it was further up-stream that the search was being carried on—and naturally, as he had just passed that way—he reached, without being recognised or pursued, the St. John River, which forms part of the boundary of New Brunswick. At St. Anne's, his daring companions were waiting for him, and on their devotion he could rely without misgiving.

They were five brothers—the eldest, Pierre and Remy, were twins, thirty years old; the three others, Michel, Tony, and Jacques, somewhat younger. They belonged to the numerous family of Thomas Harcher and his wife Catherine, of Chipogan Farm, in Laprairie county.

A few years earlier, when the rising of 1831 broke out, Jean-Sans-Nom, closely pursued by the police, had found refuge in this farm, which, though he did not know this, belonged to M. de Vaudreuil. Thomas Harcher received the fugitive into his family as though he had been one of his sons. Though he could not have failed to realise he was giving shelter to a patriot, he certainly did not know that this patriot was Jean-Sans-Nom.

While staying at the farm, Jean—he was known by no other name—had made close friends with Pierre and Remy. Their ideals responded to his. They were keen supporters of the French party, with a bitter hatred of everything that ' smelt English,' as the saying went in Lower Canada.

When Jean left Chipogan, it was on the boat in which the five brothers plied on the river from April to September. Ostensibly he too was a fisherman, and this gave him access to every house on the river-side. Thus he could baffle pursuit, and prepare a new insurrectionist movement. Before reaching the Villa Montcalm, he had visited the region of Ottawa, in Ontario. Now, as he sailed up-stream, he could give the final instructions to the folk of Lower Canada, who kept asking ' When shall we see our own people? '—thus recalling the French of long ago.

The cutter had just left St. Anne's. Although the tide

had begun to ebb, a fresh breeze from the eastward filled her sails, and the *Champlain,* as she was called, made good progress.

The climate of Canada is not so temperate as that of the United States, being very warm in summer and very cold in winter. During this first fortnight of September, the temperature was very high, and the *Champlain's* sails were filled with almost a scorching wind.

' We shall have it hot today,' commented Pierre, ' especially if the wind drops at noon.'

' Yes,' Michel added, ' and may the sun frizzle up the gnats and the black mosquitoes! There are thousands of them on this beach! '

' Brothers, this heat will soon end, and then we shall rejoice in the mildness of the Indian summer.'

It was Jean who had given his companions the fraternal title of which they were so worthy. And he was right in extolling the beauties of Canada's Indian summer, which occurs during September and October.

' Are we to fish this morning? ' asked Pierre Harcher, ' or shall we go up-stream? '

' Fish till ten,' Jean replied; ' and then we can sell our fish at Matane.'

' Then we must make for Mons Point,' replied Pierre, who was the boat's skipper. ' The water is better there, and we can return to Matane when the tide slackens.'

The sheets were shortened in, the boat luffed, and, heeling to the breeze with the stream in her favour, she headed across for Mons Point, on the north side of the river.

After an hour's sail the *Champlain* lay to, and her crew began to fish. They were skilful at their trade, having plied it all along the river, and it was seldom that their 'tides' were not extremely profitable.

This morning the gasperaux (salmon) were abundant, and more than once the nets were almost full enough to break. At ten the *Champlain* headed for Matane.

It was better to make for the southern bank of the river. On the northern bank the villages are scattered, and the people few; the land is barren, being little but a chaos of rocks, and its yield is generally poor. To the south of the river, on the contrary, the land is fertile, the villages numerous, and a succession of houses seems to extend from the river-mouth almost to Quebec.

It was to that side, to the market at Matane, that the *Champlain* brought her first load of fish, and Jean and two of the Harchers went from door to door with the product of their toil. It might have been noticed that Jean stayed at some of these houses much longer than is usual in this trade, and that he had gone right inside and exchanged a few words not only with the servants but with the masters. And it might have been noticed, too, that at some of the humbler dwellings he gave the buyers more money than his comrades had received.

The same proceedings went on during the next few days in the villages along the river. But at Rivière-du-Loup, a little town they reached on the morning of the 17th of September, the *Champlain* was boarded by the police who were watching the river. But all went well: for some years Jean had been borne on the cutter's books as if he had been one of Thomas Harchers' sons. Never would the police have suspected that under the guise of a fisherman was hidden the man they wanted, whose head was worth six thousand dollars to anyone who might betray it.

When the police had gone, Pierre Harcher remarked, ' It might be better for us to get across to the other bank.'

Michel agreed.

' But why? ' asked Jean. ' Because these men seemed to suspect our boat? Because things haven't gone on quite normally? Because they doubt that I'm one of your family? '

' As I really think you are! ' put in Jacques, a lively fellow, and the youngest of the five. ' Father has so many children that another wouldn't worry him, and he might mistake you for one of his own! '

' What's more,' Tony added, ' he loves you like a son, and we all love you as if you were of our own blood! '

' And aren't we? ' replied Remy. ' Aren't we all French? '

' Certainly! ' replied Jean. ' And that's why I don't see why you should be afraid of the police.'

' You can never be too careful,' Tony reminded him.

' Of course not,' Jean agreed, ' and if it's only for the sake of prudence that Pierre is going to cross the river . . .'

' Which it is,' said Pierre, ' for the weather will soon change.'

' That's different,' Jean replied.

' Look here,' Pierre continued, ' the north-east breeze will soon be springing up, and I have an idea it will be rather fresh. I can feel it! We must think of our boat, and I don't want to lose her on the rocks of Rivière-du-Loup or Kamour-aska! '

' All right! ' Jean replied. ' Let's put across to Tadoussac, if we can. Then we'll be able to go up the Saguenay to Chicoutimi, and then we'll lose neither our time nor our trouble.'

' Quick, then,' exclaimed Michel, ' Pierre is quite right. That north-easter isn't far off. If it catches the *Champlain* before we're across, we shall go a hundred times further towards Quebec than towards Tadoussac.'

And away went the *Champlain* to the northward, eating into a wind which at once began to freshen.

It was eight in the evening. Pierre Harcher had not been mistaken when he caught sight of the long narrow clouds that announced the coming of the storm. There was barely time to get under the shelter of the northern coast.

Five or six leagues separate Rivière-du-Loup from the mouth of the Saguenay and the crossing was rough. The wind swooped down on the *Champlain* when she was only a third of the way across. Sail had to be reduced, and every reef taken in, and yet the mast bent as if it would break. The surface of the river rose in huge waves like the sea, and the waves dashed against the cutter's bow and covered it with foam. It was rather dangerous for a boat of only a dozen tons, but the crew were steady and skilful, and more than once they had braved the storm in the open sea between Cape Breton and New-foundland. And the seamanship of the crew is as much a consideration as the seaworthiness of the ship.

But Pierre Harcher would have enough to do to reach the mouth of the Saguenay, and this would take him another three hours. When the tide ebbed it would make the sea worse, although it would keep the cutter on her course. Those who have not been caught in one of these north-easters on the St. Lawrence can have little idea of their violence. Below Quebec they are really dangerous.

Fortunately the *Champlain* found shelter under the

northern bank, and as night fell she entered the mouth of the Saguenay.

The storm had lasted only a few hours. On 19th September, at dawn, Jean could continue his propaganda along the Saguenay, and as soon as they reached Chicoutimi he got in touch with the members of the Reformist Committee. Then in the morning, taking advantage of the tide, he pushed on to Quebec.

Meanwhile, Pierre and his brothers did not forget that they were fishermen by trade. Every evening they cast their net and their lines, and in the mornings they landed at the villages on each bank.

On the southern bank special precautions had to be taken, for the surveillance on this part of the river was very strict. It would have been better, perhaps, not to have stopped at Quebec, where the cutter arrived during the evening of the 22nd. But Jean had an appointment with the lawyer Sebastien Gramont, one of the most ardent Opposition deputies.

When darkness had quite set in, Jean made his way to the upper quarters of the town, and along the Rue de Petit-Champlain to Gramont's house.

For some years the two had been in touch.

Gramont, then thirty-six years old, had taken an active part in all the political demonstrations of recent years—especially in that of 1835, for which he had been imprisoned.

It was then that he had got into touch with Jean-Sans-Nom, who had, however, told him nothing of his birth or his family. Gramont knew only one thing, that when the time came his friend would put himself at the head of the insurrection. Not having seen him since the abortive attempt of 1835, he was waiting for him tonight with a lively impatience.

When Jean arrived he was cordially welcomed.

' I've only a few hours to give you,' he said.

' Well,' replied the advocate, ' let's use them in talking about the past and the present.'

' About the past! No! ' Jean exclaimed. ' About the present—and the future—especially the future! '

Ever since he had known him Gramont had felt that Jean's life had been marked by some great misfortune, some great grief, but he had never learned what it was. As they stood face to face, Jean was so reserved that he even avoided shaking hands with him. But Gramont had never pressed him: when it suited his friend to confide in him, he would be ready to listen.

During the few hours they spent together, they discussed the political situation. The lawyer told Jean about the state of opinion in Parliament; and in return Jean described the steps already taken with a view to the rising—of the formation of a Central Committee at the Villa Montcalm, and the results of his journey through Upper and Lower Canada. He had only to traverse the Montreal district to finish his propagandist campaign.

Gramont listened very attentively; he could see real grounds for great hope in the progress the cause had made during the last few weeks: there was not a village where money had not been distributed for the purchase of arms and ammunition, and which was not waiting for the signal.

Jean then heard about the latest activities of the authorities at Quebec:

' In the first place, my dear Jean, there was a rumour that you were here a month ago. There were search warrants out for you, and even my own home was searched, it having been falsely reported that you were here. I had a visit from the detectives, and among others from a certain Rip . . .'

' Rip! ' exclaimed Jean in stifled tones, as though the name burnt his lips.

' Yes—the head of the firm of Rip and Co.,' replied Gramont. ' Remember he's a very dangerous man.'

' Dangerous! ' murmured Jean.

' And you would do well to beware of him,' added Gramont.

' To beware of him! ' Jean replied. ' Yes, to beware of him, as if he were a scoundrel.'

' Do you know him? '

' I know him,' said Jean, who had recovered his equanimity, ' but he doesn't know me yet! '

' That's the great thing! ' added Gramont, somewhat surprised at his guest's behaviour.

Then Jean, turning the conversation to another subject, asked about the proceedings in Parliament during the last few weeks.

' The opposition,' Gramont told him, ' is very strong, continually resisting the Government measures. Lord Gosford would like to prorogue the House, but he fears that it would give the signal for an uprising.'

' Would that it doesn't take place till we're ready! ' Jean replied. ' Don't let the Parliamentary leaders be imprudent enough to precipitate matters.'

' They shall be warned, and they will do nothing to interfere with your plans. At the same time, in view of a possible insurrection, the Governor-General has taken certain steps. Sir John Colborne has concentrated all the troops he has available, so as to move them quickly to the villages on the St. Lawrence, where the revolt is most likely to break out.'

' There—and at twenty other places at the same time— at least I hope so. All the French-Canadians must rise on the same day, at the same hour, so that the bureau-crats may be overwhelmed by numbers. If the movement is only local, there's a chance of its being stifled at the outset. It was to make it general that I've been travelling east and west, and that now I'm going through the central regions. I'm off this very night.'

' Go ahead then, Jean, but don't forget that the soldiers and volunteers of Sir John Colborne are concentrated round Montreal under Colonels Gore and Wetherall. It's there that we'll meet the greatest opposition.'

' We'll arrange everything so as to get all the advantage of the first shot,' said Jean. ' The Committee at the Villa Montcalm is well situated with a view to a general rising, and I know the energy of its leader, M. de Vaudreuil. In the counties adjoining Montreal, the most ardent Sons of Freedom have imparted to the towns and villages the fire of their patriotism.'

' And it's even reached the clergy! ' said Gramont. ' In public as in private, in sermons as well as private con-versations, they are preaching against the English tyranny. Only a few days ago, in the very Cathedral of Quebec, a young preacher dared to appeal to the national sentiment, and his words had such an effect that the minister of police wanted to arrest him. But Lord Gosford opposed so rigorous a measure, as he thinks he can remain good friends with the Canadian clergy. All he did was to have the bishop send the preacher away from the town, and he's carrying on his mission through the counties of Montreal. He is a real tribune of the pulpit, his eloquence is most convincing, he's held back by no personal consideration, and he will assuredly devote to our cause the sacrifice of his liberty—and his life.'

' Did you say this priest was a young man? ' asked Jean.

' He's hardly thirty.'

' What order does he belong to? '

' The Sulpiciens.'

' And his name? '

' The Abbé Joann.'

Did the name evoke any remembrance in Jean's mind? Gramont might well have thought so, for Jean remained silent for a few seconds. Then, although he had been offered hospitality till the morning, he took his leave.

' Thank you, my dear Gramont,' he said. ' But I must rejoin my companions before midnight. We must start with the tide.'

' Good-bye, then,' the lawyer replied. ' Whether your enterprise succeeds or not, you will, none the less, be one of those who have done much for our country! '

' I have done nothing, so long as she's still under the English yoke,' the young patriot declared. ' And if I can only set her free, were it at the cost of my life . . .'

' She would owe you eternal gratitude,' Gramont responded.

' She would owe me nothing! '

The friends parted. Then Jean returned to the *Champlain;* and, her anchor being weighed, she set off at once on her voyage up the river to Montreal.

CHAPTER VII

FROM QUEBEC TO MONTREAL

AT MIDNIGHT the cutter was several miles up-stream. As it was a clear moonlight night Pierre Harcher could push on quite safely, and he did not stop, except for a short pause just before dawn. A mist drowned the broad prairies, extending beyond the shore. Soon the tops of the trees in the background appeared above the mist, which the rising sun was beginning to disperse, and the river again became visible.

A number of fishermen were already at work, and the *Champlain* soon got lost among the other boats, the brothers Harcher dropping anchor on the northern shore, and setting to work with the rest of them. They needed a few baskets of fish to sell in the villages, as soon as the tide allowed them to go further up-stream in spite of the head wind.

While they were fishing, several birch-bark canoes came alongside, such light craft as a man can put on his shoulder when he has to make a portage—one of the stretches where the river is unnavigable, because of the rocks, or the falls, or rapids, or eddies so common in the Canadian rivers.

The men in the canoes were mostly Indians. They had come to buy the fish, and to take it to the towns and villages in the interior, up the numerous streams with which the land abounds. Some, however, were French-

Canadians who came alongside, and who, after a few minutes' conversation, went back to the shore to carry out the tasks with which they had been entrusted.

Had the brothers been fishing for pleasure or profit, they would have been amply satisfied, as their net and line worked wonders, and they would be heartily welcomed in the river-side houses.

The fishermen first put in-shore on the left bank, where the *Champlain* may have left more money than she received for her fish; but the Harchers made no complaint.

During the next two days Jean sailed on from shore to shore, visiting the leading advocates of reform. At Nicolet, he learned from M. Aubineau—a justice of the peace, and one of the most influential inhabitants—what he had already heard at Quebec, that the Abbé Joann was travelling through the parishes, rousing the people by his preaching. M. Aubineau also discussed the arms and ammunition they would need.

'You'll soon get them,' Jean assured him; 'a raft, which ought to have left Montreal last night, will bring you guns, and powder and shot. You'll be well-armed in good time. But take care not to rise till the signal is given. If necessary, you can get into touch with the Central Committee, at the Villa Montcalm, in Jesus Island, and with its president . . .'

'M. de Vaudreuil?'

'Yes.'

'Agreed.'

'Didn't you tell me that the Abbé Joann had passed this way?'

'He was here six days ago.'

'Do you know where he went, after he left you?'

' Into Verchères County; and, unless I'm mistaken, he was going into Laprairie County.'

Jean then took his leave of the justice of the peace, and went back on the *Champlain*, just as the Harchers returned, having sold their fish. They then crossed the river obliquely, towards St. Maurice County.

At the mouth of the river of the same name stands one of the oldest towns in the country, that of Three Rivers, at the end of a fertile valley. Here there had just been constructed a cannon-foundry, managed by a French-Canadian Company, and employing only French-Canadian workmen. Here was an anti-loyalist centre which Jean could not neglect. The *Champlain* went a few miles up the St. Maurice river, and Jean got into touch with the local committees.

The foundry, having only been recently erected, was not as yet working. A few months later it might have been able to provide the reformists with the guns they needed so bady. It was just possible, however—if they worked night and day—that the workmen could turn out the first guns in time to use them against the royal artillery. Jean had a very important discussion regarding this with the leaders of the committees: if a few of the guns could be made in time, there would be no difficulty in finding arms to serve them.

After leaving Three Rivers, the *Champlain*, on the night of 24th September, entered the widening of the St. Lawrence known at Lake St. Peter, a lake about five leagues long.

Here the Harchers cast—or rather towed—their nets, as they slowly drifted up-stream. Thick clouds covered the sky, and the darkness grew so dense that neither bank of the river could be seen.

A little after midnight, Pierre, on the look-out forward, caught sight of a light farther up-stream.

'That is a ship's light—on a drifting vessel, I think,' said Remy.

'Look after the nets,' Jacques told him. 'We have thirty fathoms out, and they'll be lost if that ship runs into them.'

'Well, starboard, then,' Michel ordered. 'There's plenty of room.'

'The wind's failing,' Pierre reminded him. 'We're drifting.'

'We'd better haul in the nets,' Tony suggested. 'That will be safer.'

'Yes, and don't let's lose any time,' Remy agreed.

The brothers were preparing to haul in the nets, when Jean asked:

'Are you certain it's a ship coming down the river?'

'I'm not sure,' Pierre replied. 'Anyhow, she's coming very slowly, and her light's almost on the water-line.'

'It may be a 'cage',' said Jacques.

'If it's a 'cage',' replied Remy, 'all the more reason for avoiding it. We must keep clear! Haul away!'

The *Champlain* might have lost her nets if the brothers had not hurried, without even stopping to remove the fish trapped in the meshes. There was not a moment to lose, for the light was only a few cable-lengths away.

A 'cage' is the name given, in Canada, to a timber-raft, composed of from sixty to seventy 'cribs' or sections, and consisting of at least a thousand cubic feet. As soon as the river is clear enough for navigation, a number of these cages descend the river every day to Montreal or Quebec. They come from the immense forests in the West, part of the inexhaustible resources of

Canada. Imagine a floating mass, five or six feet out of the water, like an enormous pontoon without any mast. It consists of tree-trunks squared by the woodmen's axes, or cut into logs and planks by the saw-mills near the waterfalls on the Ottawa. Thousands of these rafts come down the river from April to October, avoiding the falls and rapids by means of ' slides ', narrow channels dug by the side of the river. Some of the cages are stopped at Montreal, and are there loaded on ships bound for Europe, but most of them go on to Quebec.

These rafts are, as may be supposed, a great hindrance to navigation, especially in the narrow subsidiary branches of the stream. They float down with the tide, and are almost impossible to steer. Ships and fishing boats have to avoid them, as they may get damaged seriously. So it will be understood how eagerly the Harchers worked to get in their nets, which were in the way of the cage the calm would prevent them from avoiding.

Jacques was right. It was a cage with a bow-light to show the direction it was following. By the time the *Champlain* had all her nets in, it was hardly twenty fathoms away. In the silence of the night a voice could be heard singing a well-known song, whose tune is almost national. It was easy to recognise that the singer was a French-Canadian:

> ' As I came from the wedding
> I felt quite oppressed,
> And at the clear fountain
> I lay down to rest.'

Jean must have recognised the singer's voice, for he told Pierre, who was rowing his hardest to keep the *Champlain* clear, to:

' Run alongside! '

'Run alongside?' queried Pierre.

'Yes! It's Louis Lacasse.'

'We'll drift along with him!'

'Five minutes at the most,' Jean replied. 'I've only a few words to say to him.'

In a moment the helm was put down, and the *Champlain* ran alongside, and was made fast.

The man on the raft stopped singing, and shouted:

'Look out, you on that cutter!'

'There's no danger, Louis Lacasse,' said Pierre Harcher. 'It's the *Champlain*.'

Jean had jumped on the raft, and he ran up to Lacasse, who, as soon as he recognised him, said:

'My respects to you, Monsieur Jean!'

'Thank you, Lacasse.'

'I thought I should meet you, but I reckoned you'd have come when I was moored for the flood tide. But since you are here . . .'

'It's all aboard?' asked Robert.

'It's all aboard, hidden under the planks and between the logs. It's well enough stowed, I can tell you!' added Lacasse, lighting his pipe.

'Did the custom-house officers board you?'

'Yes, at Verchères. They stayed prying about for half an hour, but they saw nothing. It's shut away as safely as if it were in a box.'

'How many?' asked Jean.

'Two hundred muskets.'

'And swords?'

'Two hundred and fifty.'

'Where do they come from?'

'Vermont. Our American friends have been busy, and they haven't charged us much. But we had a lot of trouble in getting them to Fort Ontario. Now there'll be no more difficulties.'

' And ammunition? '

' Three casks of powder, and several thousand bullets. If each of them kills its man, there'll soon be not a red-coat left in Canada. Those ' frog-eaters ', as the Anglo-Saxons call us, will have eaten them! '

' You know where these things are to go? ' asked Jean.

' Yes,' Lacasse assured him. ' Never fear! There's no danger of being surprised! During the night, at low tide, I can moor my cage, and the canoes can come alongside and take their supply. But I don't go lower than Quebec, where I load my logs on to the *Moravian,* outward bound to Hamburg.'

' It's understood,' asked Jean, ' that before you reach Quebec you'll have got rid of the last gun and the last cask of powder? '

' That's right.'

' You're sure of the men you've got with you? '

' As sure as I am of myself! They're real ' Jean Baptistes ',* and when the guns begin to talk, they won't be left behind.'

Jean gave him a number of dollars, which he put into his pouch without counting them. Then after a general hand-shaking he went back on board the *Champlain,* which went off towards the left bank. And as the cage continued to float down-stream there could be heard the sonorous voice of Lacasse:

' And at the clear fountain
I lay down to rest.'

An hour later the breeze returned with the flowing tide.

---

*A name given to the French-Canadians who live in the country. —J.V.

The *Champlain* put in at the river-side villages where during the seventeenth century the women had fought so bravely against the Indians.

While the cutter stopped, Jean visited the Reformist leaders, and learned for himself the state of public opinion. Often they mentioned Jean-Sans-Nom on whose head a reward had been placed. Where was he now? Would he appear when the fight began? The patriots depended on him. In spite of the Governor-General's proclamation, he could come without misgivings into the county, and there for an hour, for twenty-four hours, all houses would be open to him.

Jean was much affected at these proofs of unswerving devotion. Yes! He was waited for like a Messiah by the French-Canadians! And then he had to confine himself to replying:

' I don't know where Jean-Sans-Nom is; but when the day comes he'll be there where he ought to be.'

About the middle of the night of 26th September, the *Champlain* was near the end of her voyage. In a few days the brothers would lay her up for the winter when navigation would become impracticable. Then Jean and his friends would go on to Laprairie County, to Chipogan Farm, where the whole family would meet for the wedding.

The skipper of the *Champlain* steered for the right bank, which he reached about five in the evening near the boundary of Laprairie county. There Jean told him:

' I must go ashore now.'

' Won't you come with us to Laprairie? ' asked Pierre.

' No. I must visit Chambly, and by landing here I shan't have so far to go.'

' There's a great deal of risk in that,' said Pierre. ' And

I shan't part with you without anxiety. Why are you leaving us, Jean? Stay a couple of days with us, and we can go away together as soon as the *Champlain* is dismantled.'

' I can't,' Jean replied; ' I've got to be at Chambly this very night.'

' Shall any of us go with you? ' asked Pierre.

' No; I must go alone.'

' And you'll stay at Chambly? '

' Only a few hours. I expect to be off again before daylight.'

As Jean did not seem to want to explain why he had to go, Pierre did not insist; he contented himself with adding:

' Shall we wait for you at Laprairie? '

' That would be useless. Do what you have to do, and don't worry about me.'

' Then we shall meet . . .'

' At Chipogan Farm.'

' You know we should all be there during the first week in October? '

' I know.'

' Don't fail to be there, Jean. Your absence would give much pain to father, my mother, and all the rest of us. We shall have a family gathering at Chipogan, and as you're one of our brothers, you must be there to make the family complete.'

' I'll be there, Pierre.'

Jean shook hands with all the brothers. Then he went into the cabin, and put on the clothes he had worn during his visit to the Villa Montcalm. A minute later he had jumped on to the bank, and with an ' au revoir ' he had disappeared under the trees whose thick masses surrounded the Iroquois village.

The brothers set to work, and with a great effort they hauled their boat up against the stream, taking advantage of the eddies sheltered by the promontories. By eight the *Champlain* was moored in a small creek at the foot of the first houses of Laprairie. The fishing season was over.

CHAPTER VIII

AN ANNIVERSARY

IT WAS five in the afternoon when Jean left the *Champlain*. He was then about three leagues from the village of Chambly, where he was going.

What was he going there for? Had he not already finished his propagandist campaign in the south-western counties before visiting at the Villa Montcalm? Yes, certainly. But he had not as yet visited this parish. Why? No one could have guessed; he had told no one, and he could scarcely have told himself. He went to Chambly as if he were being attracted there and repelled at the same time, and he fully realised the battle raging within him.

Twelve years had passed since Jean had left the village where he was born. He had never returned to it, and there was no fear of his being recognised. After so long an absence, would not he himself have forgotten the street in which stood the house in which he had passed his childhood?

No! These recollections of early life could not be effaced from so retentive a memory. As he left the riverside forest he saw himself again among the prairies which he used to cross on his way to the ferry over the St. Lawrence. He was no longer a wandering stranger, but a child of the country. He showed no hesitation in crossing some of the fords, in taking certain cross-roads and in cutting off certain corners, to shorten his route. And when he reached Chambly he would have no difficulty in recognising the little square in which stood his father's house, the narrow road by which he used to enter it, the church to which his mother had taken him, the school where he had begun his studies before he had continued them at Montreal.

Jean wanted to see once more the places he had stayed away from so long. When he was about to risk his head in a desperate struggle, an irresistible desire had taken him back to the spot where his miserable existence had commenced. It was not Jean-Sans-Nom visiting the reformists of the county, it was the boy returning, perhaps for the last time, to the village where he had been born.

Jean walked quickly, so as to reach Chambly before night and leave it before morning. Absorbed in his painful memories, his eyes saw nothing of what would normally have attracted his attention, neither the elk passing in the woods, nor the birds of a thousand kinds that flitted among the branches, nor the game which ran along the furrows.

A few labourers were still at work in the fields. He turned away so as not to have to reply to their cordial greeting, wishing to cross the country unobserved and to enter Chambly without being seen.

It was seven when he saw the church-steeple rising among the trees; a little more than a mile and he would be there. The sound of the bell was borne to him on the wind. And instead of exclaiming, ' Yes, it is I! I, who have returned to what I once loved so well—to my nest —to my cradle! ' he was silent, and asked himself in terror, ' Why have I come here? '

But the broken sound of the bell told him it could not

be the *Angelus* that was ringing. To what service, then, were the faithful of Chambly being summoned at so late an hour?

'So much the better,' Jean reflected, 'they'll be at church. I shan't have to pass the open doors; they won't see me; they won't speak to me; and as I won't ask shelter of anyone, nobody will know that I've been here.'

And he continued his journey. Then for an instant the idea of returning came to him. No. It was an invincible force which was urging him forwards.

As he neared Chambly, Jean looked about him more attentively. Notwithstanding the changes that had taken place in the last twelve years, he could recognise the houses, the yards, and the farms on the outskirts of the village.

When he reached the main street he moved past the houses, whose appearance was so French that the village might have been the capital of a seventeenth century bailiwick. Here had lived a friend of the family, with whom Jean had spent his holidays. There had lived the curé of the parish, who had given him his first lessons. Were these worthy people still alive? Then a taller building rose on the right, the school he had gone to every morning.

The road led him up to the church. His father's house had faced a corner of that square on the left, its back overlooking a garden whose trees merged into the copse surrounding the village. The night was dark. The half-open door of the church let him catch a glimpse of the interior, where a crowd was just visible in the light of the chandelier hanging from the roof.

Jean, having lost his fear of being recognised, would like to have mingled with this crowd, to have entered the church and taken part in the service, and knelt on the benches where he formerly used to pray. But at first he felt himself attracted towards the other side of the square, so he turned to the left, and reached the corner where his father's house had once stood.

He could well remember it. It was there it had been built. All its details returned to him—the gate which shut off the little front garden, the dovecot on the gable to the right, the four windows on the ground floor, the door in the middle, the window on the left of the first floor where he had so often seen his mother among the flowers that framed it. He had been fifteen when he left Chambly for the last time, but even then such details are already deeply graven on the memory. Here it was that the house should be, the house which had been built by his ancestors when the colony was founded.

But the house was gone!

In its place there was nothing but ruins. Gloomy ruins, not such as time had made, but the work of violence. There could be no mistake about that. Burnt stones, the blackened stumps of walls, charred beams, piles of ashes, white now, but recalling the time when the house had been the prey of the flames!

A horrible thought crossed Jean's mind. Who had lighted those flames? Was it the result of chance or of carelessness? Was it the hand of justice?

He was irresistibly attracted, and he entered the ruins. He stumbled against some ashes piled up on the ground.

A few owls flew off; doubtless no one ever came there. Why, then, in this most frequented part of the village, had these ruins been allowed to remain? Why, after the fire, had not the ground been cleared?

During the twelve years he had been away Jean had

never heard that the house had been destroyed, that it was now nothing but a pile of fire-blackened stones.

He stood there, his heart aching as he thought of the sorrowful past and the even more sorrowful present.

'Eh! What are you doing there, sir?' asked an old man who had just stopped on his way to church.

Jean did not hear him, and did not reply.

'Hallo!' the old man shouted. 'Are you deaf? You mustn't stop there. If they see you there, you may hear something you won't like.'

Jean came back out of the ruins on to the road, and asked:

'Were you speaking to me?'

'Yes, to you, Sir. You mustn't go in there.'

'And why not?'

'Because the place is accursed.'

'Accursed!' murmured Jean, but in so low a voice that the old man did not hear him.

'You're a stranger here, sir?'

'Yes,' said Jean.

'And you've not been to Chambly for many years?'

'Not for many years.'

'Then it isn't surprising that you don't know. Believe me, it's good advice I'm giving you—don't go back into those ruins.'

'And why?'

'Because you'll soil yourself only by treading on the cinders. It is the house of a traitor!'

'Of a traitor?'

'Yes—the house of Simon Morgaz.'

This the wretched man knew only too well!

And so, of the house from which his father had been driven twelve years ago, of the dwelling which he had wanted to see for the last time, and which he had thought would still be standing, there remained only a few flame-scorched walls. And tradition had made the place so infamous that no one dare approach it, and none of the people of Chambly could pass it without a curse! Twelve years had gone, but in this village, as throughout all Lower Canada, there had been no lessening of the horror inspired by the name of Simon Morgaz!

Jean had lowered his eyes, his hands trembling, feeling as though he would faint. Had it not been for the darkness, the old man would have seen the blush of shame that rose to his face.

' You're a French-Canadian? '

' Yes,' Jean replied.

' Then you can't be ignorant of the crime that Simon Morgaz committed? '

' Who does not know it? '

' No one, in truth. No doubt you come from the eastern counties.

' Yes—from the east—from New Brunswick.'

' That's a long way off. Perhaps you didn't know that the house had been destroyed? '

' No! An accident, probably? '

' Not at all, sir; not at all. It would have been better, perhaps, if it had been destroyed by fire from Heaven! And that will happen some day, for God is just! But we have anticipated His justice! The day after Simon Morgaz was hunted from Chambly, we burnt down his house. And that his memory might never perish we left the ruins just as you see them now. It is forbidden to go near them; and no one would soil himself with the dust of this house.'

Jean stood motionless, listening. The intensity with which the old man had spoken showed that the horror associated with Simon Morgaz was as violent as ever. Where Jean had come to look for memories of his family there were only memories of shame.

But as the old man spoke, he was moving further away from the ruins and towards the church. The bell had just stopped hurling its summons through space. The service was about to begin. Interrupted by long pauses, the chanting could already be heard, and the old man said:

' I must leave you now, sir, unless you mean to come with me to church. You'll hear a sermon that will have much influence hereabouts . . .'

' I cannot,' Jean replied, ' I have to be at Laprairie before daylight.'

' Then you have no time to lose, sir. The roads are safe enough. For some time the police have been out day and night, hunting for Jean-Sans-Nom, whom, thanks be to God, they have not yet caught. We think a good deal of that young hero, and rightly so. And if I can believe rumour, he'll find all the gallant young fellows here ready to follow him.'

' As throughout the county,' said Jean.

' Much more, sir. Haven't we to atone for the shame of having been the neighbours of Simon Morgaz? '

The old man was clearly fond of talking. But at last he was really going, and he had turned away, when Jean asked him:

' My friend, perhaps you knew the family of this Simon Morgaz? '

' I did, and quite well. I'm seventy now, and I was fifty-eight at the time of that abominable affair. What has become of him? I don't know! Perhaps he's dead. Perhaps he's gone to some foreign land, under another name, so that they cannot throw his own name in his face! But his wife, his children! Ah! how I pity the poor things! Madame Bridget I used to see so often, always good and kind through she was not very rich! All the village loved her! What she has had to suffer, poor woman—what she must have suffered! '

Who could describe what was passing in Jean's mind? Before the ruins of the house, where the last act of the treachery had been carried out, where the comrades of Simon Morgaz had been betrayed, to hear the name of his mother, to be reminded of the misery of her life, it was almost more than human nature could bear. Jean must have had an extraordinary strength of will to restrain the cry of anguish that rose to his lips.

And the old man continued:

' And I knew the two sons, sir! They took after her! Ah! the poor boys! Where are they now? Everyone here liked them for their candour and goodheartedness. The elder was more serious and studious, and the younger more lively and determined, always ready to defend the weak against the strong. His name was Jean. His brother's was Joann, just the same as that of the young preacher who's to address us tonight.'

' The Abbé Joann? ' exclaimed Jean.

' Do you know him? '

' No. But I have heard of his sermons.'

' Well, sir, if you don't know him, you ought to make his acquaintance. He has come right through the western counties, where everyone has been rushing to hear him. You'll see what enthusiasm he can arouse. If you can delay your departure an hour . . .'

' I'll come with you,' Jean decided.

With the old man he entered the church, where they had some trouble in finding seats.

The opening prayers had been said, and the preacher had just entered the pulpit.

The Abbé Joann was thirty years of age. In his impassioned face, his penetrating look, his warm, persuasive voice, he resembled his brother. In both could be traced their mother's characteristic features. To see him, or to listen to him, was to understand the influence he had over the crowd which his reputation attracted. As the spokesman of the Roman Catholic faith and the national faith, he was an apostle in the true sense of the word, a child of that brave race of missionaries who would gladly give up their lives for their religion.

The Abbé Joann began his sermon. From all that he said for his God they could feel what he wanted to say for his country. His references to conditions in Lower Canada were intended to rouse his hearers, whose patriotism only waited an opportunity for declaring itself openly. His gestures, his words, so moved his hearers, that a murmur ran through the church when he appealed to Heaven for help against the despoilers. His stirring voice sounded like a trumpet as his arm seemed to raise on high the flag of independence.

Jean, in the shadow, sat and listened. He felt as though he himself were speaking through his brother's lips. Their ideas were identical, their aspirations were identical. Both were working for their country, each in his own way, the one with words, the other with deeds, and both were equally ready to make the last sacrifice for the cause.

In these days the Catholic Clergy wielded a very real influence in Lower Canada, both from a social and from an intellectual point of view. The priests were looked upon as sacred. There was a struggle in progress between the old Catholic Faith, implanted by the French element in the colony, and the Protestant dogmas which the English sought to spread everywhere. The Catholics rallied round their curés, and the political movement that sought to wrest the Canadian provinces from the hands of the Anglo-Saxons received no slight encouragement from this alliance between the clergy and their flock.

The Abbé Joann belonged to the order of Sulpicians, which had possessed large tracts of land from the outset, and had drawn important revenues. It followed that the Sulpicians were one of the most honoured and most powerful corporations in Canada, and that their priests, as the richest landowners, were the most influential of its inhabitants.

The sermon, or rather the patriotic harangue, of the Abbé Joann, lasted about three quarters of an hour. It aroused so great an enthusiasm among the congregation that, had it not been for the sanctity of the place, it would have been greeted with long-continued applause. The heart-strings of the people had been touched by this patriotic appeal. It might be thought strange that the authorities allowed reformist propaganda to be carried on under the cloak of religion. But it would have been difficult to seize on any sentence that explicitly urged insurrection, and the pulpit enjoyed a freedom with which the Government could not lightly interfere.

The sermon over, Jean stayed in a corner of the church while the crowd flowed out. Then would he recognise the Abbé, grip his hand, exchange a few words with him, before rejoining his companions at Chipogan Farm? Yes, no doubt. The two brothers had not seen one another for several months, when they had parted each to take up his own task in the work of revolution.

Jean was waiting behind the most remote pillars of the nave, when a violent tumult could be heard outside. It seemed as though the people were manifesting their feelings of anger with extraordinary violence. At the same time there were flashes of light, which reached into the church.

The congregation trooped out, and Jean, carried on with them in spite of himself, reached the middle of the square.

What was happening?

Before the ruins of the traitor's house a great fire had just been kindled. A few men, who were soon joined by children and some of the women, were feeding the flames with armfuls of dry wood.

Cries of horror and shouts of hatred were rending the air.

' To the flames with the traitor! To the flames with Simon Morgaz! '

And then a figure of a man, clothed in rags, was dragged towards the fire.

Jean understood. The population of Chambly were going to burn Simon in effigy, just as in London they used to burn the effigy of Guy Fawkes, the criminal hero of the Gunpowder Plot.

It was the 27th of September. It was the anniversary of the day on which Walter Hodge and his companions, Clerc and Farran, had died on the scaffold.

Trembling with horror, Jean would have fled. He could not move from the ground, to which his feet seemed to be fastened. He seemed to see his father, overwhelmed with blows and insults, dragged in the mud, a prey to a delirium of hate. And he felt that all this opprobrium would recoil upon himself, Jean Morgaz.

At this very moment the Abbé Joann appeared and the crowd divided to let him pass.

He too understood the meaning of the popular demonstration. And at the same time he recognised his brother, whose livid face was lit up by the flames as a hundred voices shouted the odious date and the infamous name.

The Abbé could not restrain himself. He stretched out his arms, and rushed towards the fire as they were about to hurl the effigy into it.

' In the name of the God of mercy,' he exhorted them, ' have pity on this unhappy man's memory! Cannot God pardon every crime? '

' Not the crime of treason against one's own country, of treason against those who have fought for her! ' replied one of the men.

And in a moment the fire had devoured the effigy of Simon Morgaz, as it did at each anniversary.

The shouts redoubled, and did not cease until the fire had died away.

In the gloom no one noticed that Jean and Joann were standing, their hands clasped and their heads bowed. And then, without saying a word, they left that horrible scene, and fled from the village to which they were never to return.

CHAPTER IX

MAISON-CLOSE

IN ST. CHARLES, a small town not far from Montreal, one house stood somewhat apart from the others.

It was a humble and cheerless dwelling, consisting of only one floor, with a door and two windows facing the small weed-grown front yard. Usually the door was shut; and the windows were never open, not even behind the shutters which were always closed over them. If any daylight reached the interior, it was only through the two other windows opening on to the garden at the back.

This garden was but small, and in it grew some vegetables, a few fruit trees, pears, nuts and apples, left to the care of nature. A small yard, fenced off from the garden beside the house, contained five or six fowls, enough to provide a day's supply of eggs.

Inside, the house had only three rooms, and only such furniture as was strictly necessary. One of the rooms to the left of the entrance served as a kitchen; two others to the right were bedrooms. The narrow passage between them led from the front door to the garden.

The house was humble and sad, but this clearly was intentional; clearly, too, it was of their own choice that its occupants lived there, in poverty and humility. If a beggar should knock at the door of Maison-Close—as it was called locally—he was never allowed to depart without a small gift. Maison-Close might well have been called Maison-Charitable, for charity was there to be had at all hours.

Who lived there? A woman, always alone, dressed in black, and never without a long widow's veil. She rarely left the house—once or twice a week, only when this was essential, as on Sundays to attend Divine service. But when she went shopping she waited till nightfall or rather till evening, made her way quietly through the dark streets, and into the shop; there she spoke in a low voice and with few words, paid what was asked without attempting to bargain, and returned with her head bowed, her eyes on the ground, like a poor wretch who was ashamed to be seen. When she went to church it was at dawn to the first service, and she kept herself apart, in an obscure corner, kneeling as if absorbed in herself. Beneath her veil she kept so motionless it was almost terrifying; she would have seemed dead but for the sighs which she uttered. Occasionally some kind-hearted people would have liked to help her, would have offered their services, would have interested themselves in her, would have spoken a few words of sympathy; but she wrapped herself more closely in her widow's veil, and recoiled from them as though she were an object of horror.

The inhabitants of Saint Charles knew nothing of this stranger—or rather this recluse. Twelve years previously she had arrived in the town to take possession of this house, which had been bought on her behalf very cheaply, for its owners had been trying to sell it for some time, and had found no purchaser.

One day the townsfolk learnt that the new owner had arrived during the night, though nobody had seen her enter. Who had helped her to remove her scanty furniture, nobody knew. Never did anybody enter her house. As she lived then so had she lived ever since she had entered Saint Charles in a hermit-like isolation. The walls of Maison-Close were those of a cloister, and no one had been inside them.

But did not the townsfolk try to enquire into this woman's life, to learn her secret? At first they were somewhat astonished, and there was some gossip about the new owner of Maison-Close. They made a few wild guesses. Then they stopped wondering about her. Within her means she seemed charitable to the poor, and that counted for much in the general esteem.

Tall, bent more by grief than by age, the stranger seemed about fifty. Under the veil which fell almost to her waist was hidden a face which had once been beautiful, a high forehead, and large black eyes. Her hair was completely white, and her face seemed to have been marked with the ineffaceable tears which had filled her eyes so long. Its character, formerly gentle and smiling, now denoted sad energy and implacable will.

But had public curiosity kept careful watch on Maison-Close it would have realised that this was not absolutely closed to visitors. Three or four times a year, invariably at night, the door was opened to a stranger, or less frequently to two, who neglected no precaution in arriving and leaving unseen. Did they stay a few days in the house, or only a few hours? Nobody could say. Whenever they left, it was before dawn. Beyond doubt the woman was in touch with some member of the outside world.

It was 30th September, 1837, and eleven at night. The high road through St. Charles was then deserted, and complete darkness enshadowed the sleeping town. There was nobody to see the two men who came along the road, made their way quietly up to the wall of Maison-Close, opened the gate, which was fastened only by a latch, and knocked at the door in what was evidently a preconcerted signal.

The door was opened, and shut almost at once. The two visitors entered the first room to the right, lit by a night-lamp giving too feeble a light to be seen outside.

The woman showed no surprise at their arrival. The newcomers clasped her in their arms and kissed her forehead with filial affection.

They were Jean and Joann. The woman was their mother, Bridget Morgaz.

Twelve years before, after Simon Morgaz had been driven away by the people of Chambly, no one had doubted but that the unhappy family had left Canada to expatriate themselves somewhere in North or South America or in some distant corner of Europe. The money obtained by the traitor would enable him to live comfortably wherever he might go; and by taking another name he would escape the contempt which would have pursued him round the world.

Nothing of the sort had happened. Simon Morgaz had shot himself, and nobody suspected that his body lay in some unknown undiscoverable grave on the northern bank of Lake Ontario.

Bridget Morgaz, Jean and Joann had realised the full horror of their position. Mother and sons might be innocent of the crime of her husband and their father, but so great was the prejudice against them that they could have neither pity nor pardon. In Canada their name would be an object of universal scorn. They decided to renounce the name without thinking of taking another.

What did they want with a name, poor wretches, when the world had only scorn for them?

They · had never left the country. Before leaving Canada, they had a task to fulfil, and this task, even if they gave their lives for it, they had all three determined to accomplish.

It was to repair the wrong Simon Morgaz had done his country. Had it not been for the treason suggested by that hateful *provocateur* Rip, the plot of 1825 would have had a good chance of success. Had the Governor-General and the leaders of the British Army been kidnapped, the troops could not have been able to resist the French-Canadians, who would have risen to a man. But an act of infamy had betrayed the secret of the conspiracy, and Canada had remained under the oppressor's yoke.

Jean and Joann would take up the work interrupted by their father's treachery. Bridget, who courageously faced their terrible position, made them understand that it ought to be the object of their lives. The brothers, then seventeen and eighteen, realised their duty, and devoted themselves entirely to the work of reparation.

Bridget Morgaz was determined to live solely on her own private income, and not to keep any of the money found in the suicide's pocket-book. This money, it could only be, it must be, used for the Nationalist cause. Much of it was secretly placed in the hands of Mr. Nick, at Montreal, under the conditions already explained, but a part was kept by Jean for him to distribute direct to the Reformists. It was in this way that in 1831 and 1835 the committees had received the money they needed for the purchase of arms and ammunition. In 1837 the balance, which was still large, had just been sent to the committee at the Villa Montcalm and entrusted to M. de Vaudreuil.

Bridget had retired to the house at Saint Charles, and there her sons came in secret to visit her. For the last few years each had followed a different path to reach the same goal.

Joann, the eldest, had decided that earthly joys were not for him. His faith, intensified by the bitterness of his position, had made him decide to become a priest—but a priest militant. He had entered the Sulpician Order with the intention of upholding in his sermons the inalienable rights of his country. His natural eloquence, reinforced by the most ardent patriotism, attracted the people to him. Recently his fame had increased, and he was then at the height of his influence.

Jean had taken part in the revolutionary movement not so much by his words as by his deeds. Although rebellion had come to nothing in 1831 and 1835 his reputation had not diminished. The people looked upon him as the mysterious chief of the Sons of Liberty. The whole cause of independence seemed to be in the hands of one man, this Jean-Sans-Nom as he called himself; and it was to him alone that the patriots looked to give the signal for a new insurrection.

The hour was at hand. Before throwing themselves into this new struggle, Jean and Joann, who had met by chance at Chambly, had come to Maison-Close to see their mother, perhaps for the last time.

And now they were here with her, seated at her side. They held her hands; they spoke to her in low tones. They explained the present position: like every supreme struggle, this one would be terrible.

Bridget, imbued with the ideals with which their hearts

were full, gave herself over to the hope that at last their father's crime would be atoned for by her sons.

'My Jean, my Joann,' she told them, 'I want to share your hopes, to have faith in your success.'

'Yes, mother,' Jean assured her, 'you must have faith in it. In a few days the rising will have begun . . .'

'And may God give us the triumph a sacred cause deserves!' added Joann.

'May God help us!' Bridget replied. 'And then perhaps I shall at last have the right to pray for . . .'

Never—no, never—had a prayer yet escaped the lips of this unhappy woman for the soul of him who had been her husband.

'Mother,' Joann implored her, 'mother . . .'

'And you, my son,' said Bridget, 'have you prayed for your father, you, a priest of the God Who forgives?'

Joann bowed his head, and did not reply.

Bridget resumed:

'My sons, so far you have both done your duty; But do not forget that all you have done is only your duty. And if our country should owe to you the day of its independence, the name you once bore, the name of Morgaz . . .'

'Exists no longer!' Jean interrupted her. 'For that name no rehabilitation is possible. You can no more restore it to honour than you can restore to life the men whom our father's treason sent to the scaffold. What Joann and I are doing is not in the hope that the infamy attached to our name will disappear. That is impossible! It is not a bargain of that sort that we have made. Our one aim is to repair not the wrong done to ourselves but the wrong done to our country. Is that not so, Joann?'

'Yes,' replied the young priest. 'If God can pardon, I know that man cannot. One name will always be hated.'

' But may it not be forgotten? ' Bridget kissed her sons on their foreheads, as though she were trying to efface the indelible stain.

' Forgotten! ' Jean exclaimed. ' Go to Chambly, and you will see if it has been forgotten.'

' Jean,' Joann told him. ' Be silent! '

' No, Joann. Our mother ought to know. She has strength enough to listen, and I do not want to leave her the slightest hope that rehabilitation will ever be possible.'

And Jean, in a low voice and in broken words, explained what had happened at Chambly.

Bridget listened without a tear rising to her eyes. She could not even weep.

But was it, then, true that there was no escape? Was it possible, that the remembrance of the treason was unforgettable, and that responsibility for the crime would recoil upon the innocent? Was it written in the human conscience that the stain on the family name could never be effaced?

For some minutes not a word passed between mother and sons. They did not even look at one another. Their hands parted; they suffered acutely. Everywhere, as at Chambly, they were pariahs, outlaws, repulsed by society, and, so to speak, beyond the pale of humanity.

Towards three Jean and Joann began to think of leaving their mother. They had to go without any risk of being seen. They meant to separate, for it was essential that they must not be seen together. No one must ever know that that night the door of the Maison-Close had opened to the only visitors who ever crossed its threshold.

The brothers rose. At the moment of a separation which might be eternal they felt how strong was the tie which bound them together. Fortunately, Bridget did not realise that a reward had been offered for Jean's apprehension. Although Joann was not unaware of this, the terrible news had not yet reached the solitude of Maison-Close. Jean said nothing of it to his mother. What was the good of adding to her grief? And had not she reason enough to fear that she would never see her son again?

The moment to part had come.

' Where are you going, Joann? ' asked Bridget.

' Into the southern parishes,' said the young priest. ' There I'll wait to rejoin my brother when he's at the head of the patriots.'

' And you, Jean? '

' I'm going to Chipogan Farm, in Laprairie. There I'll find my comrades, and we'll make our final plans amid those family joys denied to ourselves, mother. Those gallant fellows have received me like a son. They'd give their lives for mine. But if they knew who I was, if they knew the name I bear! Wretches that we are, whose very touch is a pollution! But they shall not know it, neither they nor anyone else.'

Jean had fallen back into the chair, with his head in his hands, overwhelmed beneath the weight which every day bore more heavily upon him.

' Get up, brother! ' Joann spoke sternly. ' This is our expiation! Be strong enough to suffer! Get up, and let us go! '

' Where shall I see you again? ' asked Bridget.

' Not here anymore,' said Jean. ' If we win, we shall all three leave the country. We'll go far away where nobody will ever recognise us. If we give our country her freedom, it must never be known that she owes it to the sons of Simon Morgaz. No! Never! '

' And if all is lost? ' asked Bridget.

' Then, mother, you will never see us again, neither in this country nor in any other. We shall be dead! '

The brothers threw themselves for the last time into Bridget's arms. Once more the door opened and closed.

Jean and Joann walked for about a hundred yards together, and then they separated after a last look at Maison-Close, where the mother was praying for her sons.

CHAPTER X

CHIPOGAN FARM

CHIPOGAN FARM was about seven leagues from Laprairie Town, and covered a gentle rise in the ground on the right bank of a small tributary of the St. Lawrence. It was a fine property, extending over some four hundred acres, owned by M. de Vaudreuil and rented by Thomas Harcher.

In front of the house, and along the stream, lay a vast chessboard of prairie, its square fenced in geometrically; and its crops flourished on a soil consisting of a rich black mould, three or four feet thick, resting on a bed of clay.

Here there grew a variety of cereals, wheat, maize, rice, flax, hops, tobacco, and so forth. At the back of the house, and stretching out of sight beyond the hilly woodland which formed the horizon, lay a wide stretch of rich pasture, on which grazed the usual domestic animals as well as numerous horses of the vigorous Canadian breed so well esteemed by the Americans.

The forest had once covered all the country bordering on the St. Lawrence from its estuary to the great lakes. But what vast clearings have been made in them by the hand of man! What superb trees, rising a hundred and fifty feet in the air, are still falling under the thousands of axes which trouble the silence of the mighty woods where the birds swarm in myriads! The lumbermen find work—profitable but regrettable—in felling the oaks, maples, ashes, chestnuts, aspens, birches, elms, walnuts, hornbeams, pines and firs, which, sawn and trimmed, go to form the strings of rafts that descend the river. If, at the end of the eighteenth century, Cooper's heroes— Natty Bumppo, Hawkeye, the Deerslayer, or Leather- stocking—could regret the massacre of the trees, what would he have said to the pitiless destroyers who exhaust the fertility of the soil by their reckless waste?

But this reproach could not apply to the lessee of Chipogan. Thomas Harcher knew what he was about, and his men served him well. His farm deservedly bore the reputation of being a model of scientific cultivation at a time when Canadian agriculture was two centuries behind the age.

Chipogan Farm was then one of the best near Montreal. The fields were not simply allowed to lie fallow: rotation of crops saved the land from impoverish- ment. The fruit trees in the large kitchen garden were of the types that flourish in Europe, and they were cut and pruned and trained with care. As for the vegetables, the red cabbages, pumpkins, melons, sweet potatoes, bluets —the name given to the blackish bilberries eaten at dessert—there were gathered enough to supply the market at Laprairie twice a week. In short, with the hundreds of bushels of cereals, the crops of fruit and vegetables, and the thinning of the few acres of forest, the farm was a profitable investment for M. de Vandreuil, and there was no likelihood that in Thomas Harcher's hands it would become exhausted, and sink into a mere waste of weeds and briars.

The Canadian climate is well suited for agriculture. Instead of rain it has the snow which falls from the end of November to that of March, and which protects the green carpet of the fields. The keen dry cold is preferable to continual torrents. Nowhere else in the temperate zone does vegetation grow so quickly; corn sown in March is ripe in August, and hay is made in June and July. Then, as now, if there were any future on which Canada could depend, it was the farm.

The farm buildings were grouped within a palisade fence, twelve feet high. A gate with stone pillars gave the only means of access—a precaution dating from when attacks from the Indians might be expected. Now, however, the Indians were living on good terms with the colonists: two leagues to the east, at the village of Walhatta, there flourished the Huron tribe of Mahogannis, who often visited Thomas Harcher to exchange the spoils of the chase for the products of the farm.

The main farm-building consisted of a two-storey house, containing the number of rooms required by Harcher's family. One large room occupied the greater part of the ground floor between the kitchen and the larder on one side, and the apartment specially reserved for the farmer, his wife, and younger children on the other.

In the yard in front of the house, and abutting on the kitchen garden, stood the outhouses, the stables, cattle-sheds and stores; the houses and runs of the American rabbits, whose skins yield an extremely warm fabric; and the poultry yard with the prairie-chickens, who multiply more rapidly in the domesticated than in the wild state.

The large room on the ground floor was simply but comfortably furnished with articles of American manufacture. It was there that the family had their meals and passed their evenings, and this was the gathering-place for the Harchers of all ages, who liked to be together when the day's work was over. It is not surprising, therefore, that a small library held the first place, and that the second was occupied by a piano, to whose music every Sunday the boys and girls enthusiastically danced French waltzes and quadrilles.

The work of the farm required a large staff. But Thomas Harcher found enough hands in those of his own family, and did not need to employ even one hired servant.

The farmer was then in his fiftieth year. A French-Canadian by birth, he was a descendant of those hardy fishermen who had settled in Nova Scotia a century earlier. He was the perfect type of the Canadian settlers, who in North America are not called peasants but 'habitants.' Tall, broad-shouldered, powerful in body and limbs, with a strong head, greyish hair, keen-sighted, with well set teeth and a large mouth, which looked as if it belonged to someone who needed an ample supply of food, and a good-tempered, frank expression, he had made many firm friends in the neighbouring parishes. Moreover as a good patriot he was an implacable enemy of the English, always ready to do his duty even at the cost of his life.

He would have sought in vain throughout the St. Lawrence Valley for a better comrade than his wife, Catherine. She was then about forty-five, as strong as her husband, and like himself young in body and spirit, a little rough, perhaps, in features and bearing, but good-natured and brave, and as much the ' mother ' as he was the ' father ', in every sense of the word. They were an excellent couple, and so healthy that they promised to live to a hundred, for the Canadian climate is very conducive to longevity.

One reproach, perhaps, might be levelled at Catherine Harcher, but it was one she shared with all the women of the district, who are excellent housekeepers on condition that their husbands clean the house, make the beds, lay the table, pluck the fowls, milk the cows, churn the butter, peel the potatoes, light the fires, wash the crockery, dress the children, clean the furniture, and do the washing. However, Catherine did not push to the extreme that spirit of domination which in most of the French-Canadian houses makes the husband the wife's slave. To be just, it should be said that she did her share of the daily work. Nevertheless Thomas Harcher willingly submitted to her wishes and whims, and a fine family she had given him, ranging from Pierre, master of the *Champlain* and the first-born, down to the last baby, aged only a few weeks, who was soon to be christened. In Canada the fertility of marriage is really extraordinary. Families of twelve and fifteen are quite common, those of twenty are not rare, and even those of twenty-five are occasionally heard of. It is not so much the family as the tribe which develops under the influence of the patriarchal customs.

If Ishmael Bush, Fenimore Cooper's old pioneer in *The Prairie*, could point with pride to his seven sons, not counting his daughters, the issue of his marriage with the robust Esther, with what a feeling of superiority Thomas Harcher would have overwhelmed him—the father of twenty-six children, all very much alive at Chipogan Farm!

Fifteen sons and eleven daughters, of all ages within a few weeks of thirty. Of the fifteen sons four, and of the eleven girls two, were married, and with the seventeen grandchildren of their marriages and their mothers and fathers, the Harcher family numbered just fifty-two in the direct line!

The five eldest formed the crew of the *Champlain,* the devoted companions of Jean. No need to waste time on the names of the other children, or on their individual character. Sons, daughters, grandsons and granddaughters, these never left the farm. They worked upon it under the direction of their chief. Some were in the fields, where work never failed them. Some were in the woods, employed as lumbermen, and they too had plenty to do. Two or three went hunting in the forests near Chipogan, and furnished the game for the large family table. In these woods there still abounded elk, cariboo— a kind of large reindeer—bison, deer, roebuck, and a diversity of smaller game, furred and feathered, divers, wild geese, ducks, woodcock, snipe, partridges, quail and plover.

Pierre Harcher and his brothers, Remy, Michel, Tony and Jacques, when the cold forced them to leave the waters of the St. Lawrence, came to winter at the farm, and went fur-hunting. They were among the most intrepid and indefatigable of the backwoodsmen, and they sent their furs to the markets of Montreal and Quebec. At that time, much of the game had not yet gone off towards the north, and there was a good trade in furs, for there was as yet no need to travel in search of these to the distant shores of Hudson's Bay.

To lodge all this family of children and grandchildren a barracks would not have been too large, and the huge building also contained a few spare rooms for the guests that Thomas Harcher occasionally received, county friends, farmers of the vicinity, and voyageurs who worked the rafts down the tributaries to the main river. There, too, were rooms reserved for M. de Vaudreuil and his daughter when he came to visit the farmer's family.

It was on 5th October that these had arrived. It was not only a business relationship which united M. de Vaudreuil and Thomas Harcher, it was also a reciprocal affection, of friendship on one side and devotion on the other, which had not failed for many years. And how closely were they bound, above all, by their politics, for the farmer and his landlord were devoted body and soul to the Nationalist cause.

The family was now complete. Three days previously Pierre and his brothers had left the cutter dismantled at Laprairie, and taken up their winter quarters at the farm. There was now only one absentee: the adopted son, who was not the least loved of those who dwelt at Chipogan.

But Jean was expected that very day. If he did not arrive it would be because he had fallen into the hands of the emissaries of Rip, and the news of his arrest would soon have spread throughout the country. He had a duty to perform, as sacred to him as it was to Thomas Harcher.

The time was not far distant when the lord of the manor would be godfather to all the children of his tenants, and these might be counted by hundreds. So far M. de Vaudreuil had acted for only two of the farmer's family. Now it was Clary who was to be godmother to the twenty-sixth child, and Jean was to be godfather. And the girl was pleased at this bond which would unite them for a few short moments.

It was not only for a christening, however, that the farm of Chipogan was to keep holiday.

When Thomas Harcher received his five sons, ' My

boys,' he said, ' you're welcome. You've come at a good time.'

' As we always do, father,' said Jacques.

' No, better than usual. If today we are gathered together for the christening of the latest baby, tomorrow there is to be the first communion of Clement and Cecile, and next day the wedding of your sister Rose with Bernard Miquelon.'

' Things are going well in our family! ' exclaimed Tony.

' Yes, not bad, my boys,' said the farmer, ' and it isn't unlikely that next year I'll call you altogether for another of these events.'

And Thomas Harcher gave a hearty laugh, while Catherine kissed the five stalwart boys, the oldest in her family.

The christening was to take place at three in the afternoon. As soon as Jean arrived they would go in procession to the parish church, about more than half a league away.

Thomas, his wife, his sons, his daughters, his sons-in-law and his daughters-in-law, and his grandchildren, had all donned their best clothes for the occasion, and did not seem likely to change into any others for the next three days. The daughters had white bodices and glaringly-coloured skirts, with their hair floating over their shoulders. The sons had put off their everyday clothes and their Norman caps, and wore their Sunday costume, including a black hooded cloak, parti-coloured belt, and shoes of plaited sowskin.

On the previous evening M. and Mlle. de Vaudreuil had taken the boat across the St. Lawrence opposite Laprairie, and had been met by Thomas Harcher, who had brought them on in the buggy drawn by three spirited ' trotters.'

On the way the landlord had warned the farmer that he must be on his guard. The police were sure that de Vaudreuil had left the Villa Montcalm, and it was quite possible that he was the object of special surveillance.

' We'll keep our eyes open, master,' said Harcher, in whose use of the word there was nothing servile.

' So far you've seen nothing suspicious in the neighbourhood? '

' Not even a Canouache! '*

' And your adopted son,' said Clary, ' has he arrived at the farm? '

' Not yet; and that makes me anxious.'

' Since he left his companions at Laprairie you haven't had any news? '

' None.'

And since the visitors had been ushered into the two best rooms of the farm, Jean had not arrived. Yet, everything had been prepared for the baptism, and if the godfather did not arrive during the afternoon they would be at a loss what to do.

Pierre and two or three of the others had gone a good league down the road to meet him. But Jean had not yet been seen, and twelve was just about to strike.

Thomas and Catherine were discussing this together.

' What shall we do, if he doesn't come before three? ' asked the farmer.

' We'll wait,' said Catherine.

' What shall we wait for? '

---

*A term of contempt which the Canadians use for certain of the Indian tribes of the west.—J.V.

' Well, not for the arrival of our twenty-seventh! ' she retorted.

' And how many more? '

' You're joking, Monsieur Harcher.'

' I'm not joking! But if Jean is too late, we may have to do without him.'

' Do without him!' exclaimed Catherine. ' Never! I told him he should be godfather to one of our children, and we'll wait until he comes.'

' But if he doesn't come? ' Thomas could not understand the christening being put off indefinitely. ' If something has happened to make it impossible for him to come . . .'

' No evil prophesying, Thomas,' said Catherine. ' If we don't hold the christening today, we can hold it tomorrow, I suppose? '

' But tomorrow is the first communion of Clement and Cecile, our sixteenth and seventeenth? '

' Well, the day after? '

' That's the wedding-day of Rose with Bernard Miquelon! '

' That's enough, Thomas! We can do them all at once if we have to. But when a baby has the chance of having a godfather like Jean, and a godmother like Mademoiselle Clary, we needn't be in a hurry to get substitutes! '

' But the curé has been told! ' Thomas protested.

' That's my business,' said Catherine. ' Our curé is an excellent man, and he shan't lose his fee; and he wouldn't like to disoblige clients like us! '

And certainly there were few of his parishioners who gave him so much to do as did Thomas and Catherine.

As time went by the anxiety grew greater. If the Harchers did not know that their adopted son was Jean-

Sans-Nom, the Vaudreuils did, and they were deeply concerned about him.

So they asked Pierre Harcher under what circumstances Jean had left the *Champlain*.

' It was at Caughnawaga we landed him,' replied Pierre.

' When? '

' On the twenty-sixth of September, about five in the afternoon.'

' Then he's been away for nine days? ' asked M. de Vaudreuil.

' Yes, nine days! '

' And he didn't say what he was going to do? '

' He meant ' explained Pierre, ' to visit Chambly, where he hadn't been during the whole of our fishing cruise.'

' Yes, that's a reason,' agreed M. de Vaudreuil. ' But I'm sorry he ventured alone in a place where the police are sure to be on the look-out.'

' I offered to let Jacques and Tony go with him,' added Pierre; ' but he refused.'

' And what's your idea about all this? ' asked Clary.

' My idea is that Jean had long meant to go to Chambly, but that he'd said nothing about it to us. As we had agreed to land at Laprairie and meet here at the farm, he didn't tell us until we were off Caughnawaga.'

' And when he went away, did he promise to be here for the christening? '

' Yes,' said Pierre; ' he knew that without him the family wouldn't be complete.'

After this formal promise the only thing to do was to wait.

But if the day went by and Jean did not appear, alarm would be justifiable. For so resolute a man not to appear

on the appointed day meant that the police had got hold
of him. And then, as M. and Mlle. de Vaudreuil knew
only too well, he was lost.

Suddenly the gate in the fence opened, and a savage
appeared.

A savage—for in Lower Canada all Indians are so
called, even in official documents.

The savage was a Huron, and of pure race—as was
obvious from his beardless face, hs prominent cheek-
bones, his small gleaming eyes. His tall stature, his quick
penetrating glance, the colour of his skin, the arrange-
ment of his hair, made him recognisable as an indigenous
American.

The Huron was clothed almost in the Canadian
manner, for though the Indians cling to their ancient
rights they have in certain respects adopted the customs
of the pale-faces, and only in special circumstances do
they wear their traditional costume and their war-paint.
He belonged to the Mahogannis Tribe, who occupied a
village of fourteen or fifteen fires in the north.

' What can I do for you, Huron? ' asked Thomas
Harcher as the Indian advanced and solemnly shook
hands.

' Will Thomas Harcher reply to the question I will ask
him? ' replied the Huron, in the guttural tone
characteristic of his race

' And why not,' asked the farmer, ' if my reply will
interest you? '

' Then my brother will listen, and judge what he ought
to say.'

Only by this turn of speech, in which the savage asks
in the third person, with the most dignified air, probably
for some very simple information, there can be recognised

the descendant of the four great nations who formerly possessed the territory of North America: the Algonquins, Hurons, Montagnais, and Iroquois. Now, however, there remained only the scattered fragments of the ancient races.

After a short silence, the Indian, with an imposing gesture, spoke again:

' My brother doubtless knows the lawyer, Nicholas Sagamore, of Montreal? '

' I have that honour.'

' Is he not coming to the farm of Chipogan? '

' That is true.'

' Can my brother inform me if Nicholas Sagamore has arrived? '

' Not yet,' said Thomas Harcher. ' We don't expect him till tomorrow, to draw up the marriage settlements between my daughter Rose and Bernard Miquelon.'

' I thank my brother for the information.'

' Have you anything important to say to Mr. Nick? '

' Very important,' replied the Huron. ' Tomorrow the warriors of my tribe will leave our village of Walhatta and come to visit him.'

' You will be welcome at Chipogan,' Thomas Harcher said.

And thereupon the Indian stretched out his hand to the farmer and solemnly withdrew.

A quarter of an hour later the gate was again opened. This time it was Jean, whose arrival was welcomed with shouts of joy.

Thomas and Catherine Harcher, their children and grandchildren, rushed up to him, and it took him some time to reply to the greetings of all those who were so

pleased to see him again. Handshakes and kisses took up
a full five minutes.

Time was pressing, and M. de Vaudreuil, Clary and
Jean could exchange only a few words. But as they were
to pass three days at the farm together, they would have
leisure enough to talk later on. Thomas Harcher and his
wife were in a hurry to get to the church, as they did not
want to keep the curé waiting. The godfather and godmother were ready, and it was time to start.

' Let's get away,' Catherine was going from one to the
other, scolding and ordering them about. ' Come along,
my son,' she told Jean, ' Give your arm to Mademoiselle
Clary. And Thomas? Where's Thomas? There'll be no
end to this! Where's Thomas? '

' Here I am, wife.'

' You've got to carry the baby.'

' All right.'

' And don't let him fall.'

' All right. I've carried twenty-five to the curé, and now
I've got into the way of it.'

' That'll do!' Catherine interrupted. ' Let's be off.'

So the procession left the farm. At its head was
Thomas, with the baby in his arms, and Catherine beside
him. M. de Vaudreuil, his daughter, and Jean came next;
then followed the family of three generations, in which
the ages had become so intermixed that the baby just
born had many nephews and nieces older than himself
among the children of his brothers and sisters.

It was a bright, sunshiny day, but at this time of the
year the temperature would have been rather low if the
sun had been hidden by the clouds. The procession
passed under the trees, along the winding footpath at
whose end rose the church spire. A carpet of dry leaves

covered the ground. The autumnal tints were thick on the chestnuts, birches, oaks, beeches, aspens, some of which had their branches bare, while the firs and pines stll retained their foliage of green.

As the procession passed on, several friends of Thomas Harcher, farmers in the neighbourhood, joined in. And it was quite a hundred strong when it reached the church, including a few strangers who had been attracted by curiosity or idleness.

Among the strangers, Pierre Harcher noticed a man whose manner aroused his suspicions, and who had plainly come from a distance. Pierre had never seen him before, and he got the impression that the intruder was taking stock of the farmer's family.

Pierre had good reason to mistrust the man. He was one of the police-officers who had received orders to keep an eye on M. de Vaudreuil since he left the Villa Montcalm. Rip, still hunting for Jean-Sans-Nom, whom he believed to be hidden in the suburbs of Montreal, had given the man orders to watch not only M. de Vaudreuil, but also the Harcher family, of whose Reformist opinions he was well aware.

As they walked side by side, M. de Vaudreuil and his daughter and Jean talked over the reasons for the latter's delay in reaching the farm.

' I heard from Pierre,' said Clary, ' that you had left him to go to Chambly and the neighbouring parishes.'

' Quite so,' Jean agreed.

' Did you come here straight from Chambly? '

' No; I had to go into St. Hyacinthe, and I could not get back at once, as I had hoped. I had to go a long way round . . ."

'Were the police on your track?' asked M. de Vaudreuil.

'Yes,' said Jean; 'but with a little difficulty I managed to elude them.'

'Every hour of your life you are in danger,' said Mlle. de Vaudreuil. 'There isn't a moment but your friends tremble for you. Since you left the Villa Montcalm our anxiety has never ceased.'

'That,' Jean explained, 'is why I'm so eager to end this life which I have to fight for so unceasingly, that's why I'm so eager to act in broad daylight face to face with the foe! Yes! the time has come when the battle should begin! But at this moment let's forget the future for the present. This is a truce, a halt before the battle! Here, Monsieur de Vaudreuil, I am simply the adopted son of this brave and honest family.'

The procession had arrived, and the little church could hardly hold the crowd.

The curé was on the threshold, near the modest stone font which served for the baptismal ceremonies of the many newly-born of the parish.

Thomas Harcher presented, not without some pride, the twenty-sixth offspring of his marriage with the no less proud Catherine. Clary de Vaudreuil and Jean stood side by side while the curé went through the accustomed ceremony.

'And you name this child?' he asked.

'Jean, like his godfather!' said Thomas Harcher, extending his hand to the young man.

One of the ancient customs of France still exists in the towns and villages of Lower Canada. In the rural parishes the Catholic clergy are supported by the so-called tithes, but the tithe there is the twenty-sixth of the fruit and crops of the land, and by a strange tradition this twenty-sixth is not confined only to the crops.

And so Thomas Harcher was not astonished, when the baptism was over, to hear the curé say, in a loud voice:

' This child belongs to the Church, Thomas Harcher. He may be the godson of the godfather and godmother you have chosen, but he is my pupil! Are not children the fruit of the family? As you have given me the twenty-sixth part of your corn harvest, it is the twenty-sixth of your children which is given to the Church this day! '

' We recognise your right,' replied Thomas Harcher, ' and my wife and I submit to it with good grace.'

The child was then taken to the presbytery, where he was warmly welcomed.

Henceforth, by the tradition of the tithe, little Jean belonged to the Church, and as such he would be brought up at the expense of the parish.

And when the procession was formed to return to the farm of Chipogan there were renewed outbursts of cheers in honour of Thomas and Catherine Harcher.

CHAPTER XI

THE LAST OF THE SAGAMORES

NEXT DAY the ceremonies continued. There was another procession to the church, with the same welcome when it arrived and the same excitement on the way back.

Young Clement and Cecile Harcher, the one in his black coat and looking like a little man, the other in her white dress and looking like a little bride, were among those making their first Communion from the local farms. Though the other ' habitants ' were not as rich in offspring as Thomas Harcher of Chipogan, yet they had quite a respectable number of olive branches. Laprairie County was full of blessings from the Lord, and could vie with the most prolific villages of Nova Scotia.

This day Pierre saw no more of the stranger whose presence had given him some anxiety the previous day. The detective had disappeared. Had he any suspicions regarding Jean-Sans-Nom? Had he gone to report to his chief at Montreal? Doubtless they would soon know.

When the family returned to the farm, their chief business was to do justice to the luncheon. Everything was ready, thanks to the multifarious instructions Thomas Harcher had received from Catherine. He had to see to the table, the kitchen, the cellar, with the help of his sons who, needless to say, had their share of the maternal scoldings.

147

'It's as well for them to get used to it,' said Catherine. 'It'll come more natural to them when they have homes of their own.'

And it really was a good apprenticeship.

But if the luncheon of the day took so much seeing to, what about that of the morrow? A table to be laid for a hundred? Yes! that was the number, taking into account the bridegroom's friends, not to mention Mr. Nick and his clerk, who would attend for the signing of the marriage settlements. An incomparable wedding indeed!

But that was for tomorrow. Today all that could be done was to welcome the lawyer, and one of the Harchers had gone off to Laprairie with the buggy to bring him at three.

Catherine remembered that Mr. Nick was a hearty eater as well as a gourmet, and she did not expect—this was one of her ways of keeping her menfolk in order—that his food would be quite to his liking.

'It'll be all right,' the farmer assured her. 'You can take things easily, Catherine.'

'I shan't take things easily,' Catherine retorted. 'Not till everything's over. There's sure to be something wanting at the last moment, and I won't hear of that.'

Thomas Harcher went on with his work muttering:

'A splendid woman! A little fussy, no doubt. She won't hear of this! She won't hear of that! And yet she isn't at all deaf! '

M. de Vaudreuil and Clary had had a long conversation with Jean about his journey through Lower Canada. They told him what had happened after he left: Farran, Clerc, and Hodge had often been to the Villa, as had the lawyer Gramont, who had then gone to Quebec to find the principal opposition Deputies.

After luncheon M. de Vaudreuil had gone in the buggy to confer with the president of the Laprairie Committee and return with the lawyer.

His daughter and Jean accompanied him along the lovely elm-shaded road from Chipogan, alongside one of the smaller tributaries of the St. Lawrence. He had started before the buggy, and was not overtaken till he was half a league from the farm, whereupon Clary descended and her father took his seat by Pierre Harcher, soon to disappear at a rapid trot.

Jean and Clary returned through the quiet tranquil woods beside the stream. Here there was nothing to hinder them, neither undergrowth nor branches, which in Canadian forests grow upwards. From time to time the lumberman's axe resounded as it fell upon some tree-trunk; shots could be heard in the distance, and occasionally a couple of deer would appear amid the bushes, which they cleared at a bound. But hunters and lumbermen were hidden in the thickets, and it was through a complete solitude that the two walked slowly towards the farm.

They were soon to separate. Where and when would they meet again? Their hearts sank at the thought of the coming parting.

'Do you think you'll be coming back to the Villa Montcalm?' asked Clary.

'As M. de Vaudreuil's house it will be carefully watched,' Jean replied. 'And for his sake it would be better for me to keep our friendship secret.'

'But you're not going to take refuge in Montreal?'

'No, although it would be easy to avoid pursuit in so large a town. Still, I should be safer with Vincent Hodge, or Farran or Clerc, than in the Villa Montcalm.'

' But not more welcome! '

' I know that, and I shall never forget that during the few days I spent with you, your father and you treated me like a son, like a brother! '

' And so we should,' Clary insisted. ' To be united by the same bond of patriotism is to be united by the same blood. I sometimes feel as though you'd always been one of our family. And now if you are alone in the world . . .'

' Alone in the world,' Jean hung his head. ' Yes—alone —alone.'

' Well, after our cause triumphs, our home will be yours! But meanwhile I quite understand that you need a safer retreat than the Villa Montcalm. You will find it, for where is the French-Canadian who would shut his door against a fugitive? '

' Nowhere that I know of,' said Jean, ' and there is not one of them who would betray me.'

' Betray you! ' exclaimed Mademoiselle de Vaudreuil. ' No! The time for treason has passed! In all Canada we shall never again see a Simon Morgaz! '

Uttered with such horror, the name made the blush rise to the young man's forehead, and he had to turn away to hide his distress. Clary had not noticed this; but when he returned, his face betrayed such suffering that she asked anxiously:

' My God, what is the matter with you? '

' Nothing,' he reassured her, ' nothing. A weakness to which I'm occasionally subject! I felt as though my heart would burst, but it's over now! '

Clary looked at him as if she were trying to read his innermost thoughts.

To change the conversation so distressing for himself, he continued:

'The best thing for me to do would be to take refuge somewhere in the neighbourhood where I can keep in touch with M. de Vaudreuil and his friends.'

'But without going far from Montreal?'

'No, for probably it will be in your neighbourhood that the insurrection will break out. Anyhow, it doesn't much matter where I go.'

'Perhaps,' said Clary, 'Chipogan Farm might still be safest.'

'Perhaps.'

'It would be hard to find you among the farmer's numerous family.'

'Maybe, but if that did happen, it might have serious consequences for Thomas Harcher! He doesn't know that I am Jean-Sans-Nom, with a price on his head!'

'Do you think for a moment,' asked Clary, 'that he'd hesitate if you were to tell him?'

'No, he would not,' Jean declared. 'He and his sons are patriots, as I realised quite well while we were together on our propagandist work. But I wouldn't like Thomas Harcher to become a victim for my sake. And if the police were to find me at his farm, they'd arrest him. I'd rather give myself up.'

'Give yourself up!' Clary's voice showed her distress.

Jean lowered his head. He understood only too well the nature of the feelings to which, almost in spite of himself, he had given way. He felt the chain that was binding him ever more closely to Clary de Vaudreuil. But could he love her? The love of a son of Simon Morgaz! How disgusting! And what treachery, too, for he could never tell her the name of the family from which he came! No! He must go away and never see her again!

When he had recovered his self-control, he said:

' Tomorrow night I shall have left Chipogan Farm, and I shan't reappear until the hour of the struggle. Then I shan't have to hide! '

His features showed a trace of excitement, then they resumed their habitual calm.

Clary looked at him with an indefinable expression of sorrow. She would have liked to ask him about his former life. But how could she without paining him by some indiscreet question?

However, after giving him her hand, which he only touched lightly, she said:

' Jean, forgive me if my sympathy for you makes me seem intrusive. There's some mystery in your life—some misfortune! You must have suffered terribly? '

' Terribly! ' said Jean.

And as if he had spoken against his will, he at once added:

' Yes, I suffered terribly, because I haven't been able to give my country what she has the right to expect from me.'

' The right to expect,' Clary sounded incredulous, ' the right to expect from you? '

' Yes, from me,' said Jean, ' as from all other Canadians, whose duty it is to sacrifice themselves to give their country her freedom.'

Clary realised what a burden of sorrow was hidden beneath these patriotic words. She would have liked to know what it was, so that she could share it, could lighten it, perhaps! But how could she if Jean persisted in these evasive replies? Yet she thought she could at least say:

' Jean, I hope the national cause will soon triumph!

Its triumph will be chiefly due to your devotion, your courage, the ardour you've imparted to its supporters. It's only right that they should know whom they owe it to.'

'Know that?' Jean started away from her. No, never!'

'Never? If the French-Canadians to whom you've restored their freedom ask you to stay at their head.'

'I should refuse!'

'You could not!'

'I should refuse, I tell you!' His tone was so positive that Clary was silent. Then he added more gently:

'Clary de Vaudreuil, we cannot read the future. I hope that events will turn out to the advantage of our cause. But it would be better for me to die in its defence!'

'To die! You!' Clary's eyes filled with tears. 'To die, Jean! But your friends?'

'Friends? My Friends? Mine?'

And his expression was that of some unhappy wretch, who through some shameful event in his life had been placed under the ban of humanity.

'Jean,' Clary tried to comfort him. 'You must have suffered in the past, and you are suffering now! And what makes your position all the more sad is that you cannot—or rather you will not—confide in anyone, not even in me, who would so willingly bear some of your burden. Well, I can wait, and I can only ask you to believe in my friendship.'

'Your friendship!' murmured Jean; and he recoiled, as though his very friendship might soil her purity.

But was not the one consolation that would enable him to bear his frightful life, the friendship of Clary de Vaudreuil? When he was at the Villa Montcalm he had

felt his own heart full of the ardent sympathy which he
had inspired in her, and which he felt for her. But, no!
It was impossible! Unhappy wretch! If Clary were ever
to learn whose son he was, she would recoil from him in
horror! A Morgaz! Yes, as he had told his mother, if
he and Joann were to survive this last effort they would
disappear! Yes, once their duty were accomplished, the
dishonoured family would go far away, so far away that
nobody would ever hear of them again.

Silently and sadly they went back together to the farm.

At about four there was a great uproar at the gate. The
buggy was returning, announced from afar by the shouts
of joy with which the guests welcomed the arrival of M.
de Vaudreuil, Mr. Nick and his young clerk.

What a welcome they gave to the lawyer, and how well
he deserved it, so glad they were to have him at Chipogan
Farm.

' Mr. Nick! How are you, Mr. Nick? ' exclaimed the
elders, while the younger members of the family hugged
him in their arms, and the little ones danced round him.

' Yes, my friends, here I am! ' he smiled. ' It really is
me, and nobody else! But steady! You don't have to
tear my coat off my back, I assure you.'

' Now, children, leave him alone,' Catherine told them.

' Indeed,' the lawyer continued. ' I'm delighted to see
you, and to be here with my dear client, Thomas
Harcher.'

' Mr. Nick,' the farmer responded, ' it's very kind of
you to come! '

' And I'd have come much farther, from the end of
the world if I had to, from the sun, from the stars—yes,
Thomas, from the stars! '

' It's an honour for us, Mr. Nick,' Catherine motioned

to her eleven daughters to drop a curtsey.

' And for me,' Mr. Nick replied, ' it's a pleasure! Ah, Madame Catherine, you're as charming as ever! When are you going to stop getting younger? '

' Never! never! ' chorused her fifteen sons.

' I must have a kiss, Madame Catherine! ' Mr. Nick declared. ' You'll allow me? ' he asked the farmer, after he had bestowed a loud smack on the lady's cheeks.

' As often as you like,' Thomas Harcher assured him.

' Now it's your turn, Lionel,' added the notary. ' Kiss Madame Catherine! '

' Gladly,' smiled Lionel, as he received a double kiss in exchange for his own.

' And now,' went on Mr. Nick, ' I hope the charming Rose will be happy. How often I used to give her rides on my knee when she was young. Where is she? '

' Here I am, Mr. Nick,' Rose was abloom with health and good humour.

' Yes, you really are charming,' the lawyer complimented her, ' and so charming that I really must plant a kiss on each of those cheeks, so worthy of the name they bear! '

And he kissed them well and truly. But this time—very much to his regret—Lionel was not invited to share in the tribute.

' Where's her intended? ' asked Mr. Nick. ' Has he forgotten the day? Where is he? '

' Here,' replied Bernard Miquelon.

' Ah! he's a fine lad, a good-natured lad! ' exclaimed Mr. Nick. ' I'd like to kiss him too, to complete . . .'

' Come on, Mr. Nick,' the young man opened his arms.

' Good! ' but Mr. Nick shook his head. ' I fancy that

Bernard Miquelon would rather have one kiss from Rose than two from me! And so, Rose, give your future husband a kiss from me! '

Which Rose rather confusedly did, amid the applause of the whole family.

' Well,' said Catherine, ' I'm sure you must be thirsty, Mr. Nick, and your clerk too.'

' Very thirsty,' said Mr. Nick, and Lionel heartily agreed.

' Now, Thomas, what are you looking at? Get on with your work! Go and get a good drink for Mr. Nick, and devil take it, another for his clerk? Do I have to ask you twice? '

No! Once was enough, and the farmer hurried off, followed by two or three of his daughters, while Mr. Nick, who had just caught sight of Clary de Vaudreuil, went over to speak to her.

' Well, my dear young lady, at the last visit I paid to the Villa Montcalm we made an appointment to meet at the farm of Chipogan, and I'm happy . . .'

He was interrupted by an exclamation from Lionel, whose surprise was only natural. Was he not facing that young stranger who had so sympathetically received his poetical effort a few weeks before?

' But, it is Monsieur—Monsieur . . .' he repeated. M. de Vaudreuil and Clary looked at each other anxiously. How did Lionel know Jean? And if he knew him, did he know that the Harchers did not know they were giving shelter to Jean-Sans-Nom?

' Quite so,' the lawyer turned to the young man. ' I can remember you, Monsieur! You were our travelling companion, when my clerk and I were going in the buggy to the Villa Montcalm at the beginning of September.'

'That's right, Mr. Nick,' Jean agreed, 'and it's with real pleasure, believe me, that I find you here, along with our young poet.'

'Whose poem received an honourable mention at the Lyre Amicale!' the lawyer added. 'It's evidently a nursling of the Muses that I keep in my office to draw up my deeds!'

'Please accept my compliments, my young friend,' said Jean. 'I haven't forgotten your charming lines:

'To be born with you, my frolicsome flame,

    To die with you, my will-o'-the-wisp.'

'Ah, monsieur!' Lionel felt very proud of this praise, and that two of his lines had lingered in the memory of so good a judge.

On hearing this exchange of compliments Clary and her father were greatly relieved. Mr. Nick then explained how they had met Jean on the way from Montreal, and Jean was introduced to Mr. Nick and his clerk as the adopted son of the Harchers. The explanations ended by a hearty hand-shake all round.

Then Catherine's imperious voice could be heard:

'Now then, Thomas! Come along! Will you never get that drink? Are you going to let Mr. Nick and Mr. Lionel die of thirst?'

'It's ready, Catherine, it's ready!' the farmer protested. 'Don't be so impatient!'

And he invited the lawyer to follow him into the dining-room.

Neither Mr. Nick nor Lionel wanted much pressing. Taking their places at a table on which were some coloured cups, and napkins of dazzling whiteness, they refreshed themselves with toddy, a pleasant beverage consisting of gin, sugar and cinnamon, and flanked with some crisp toast—a little snack to enable them to wait till dinner-time without fainting.

Then they all set to work on the last preparations for the next day's festival, which would doubtless be long remembered at Chipogan Farm.

Mr. Nick strolled about, chatting. He had a kind word for everyone, while M. de Vaudreuil, Clary and Jean discussed more serious matters as they walked under the trees in the garden.

By about five all the relatives and guests were assembled in the larger room for the signing of the marriage contract. Mr. Nick of course presided at this important ceremony, and the due dignity and notarial grace he showed can well be imagined.

The wedding presents were then given to the young couple. Not one of the brothers or brothers-in-law, not one of the sisters or sisters-in-law, but had made some purchase for Rose Harcher and Bernard Miquelon. And so numerous were the useful articles and the ornaments that the young couple could well have set up house-keeping on them. But when Rose had become Madame Miquelon she was not thinking of leaving Chipogan. Bernard and the children would simply be a welcome increase to Thomas Harcher's family.

The most valuable presents were given by M. de Vaudreuil and his daughter: for Bernard Miquelon there was an excellent gun that rivalled Leatherstocking's favourite weapon, Rose had a necklace which made her look more charming than ever. Jean gave his comrades' sister a work-basket that was certain to delight a good housewife.

And at each gift there were hand-claps and shouts of applause which were redoubled when Mr. Nick solemnly placed on the young couple's fingers their wedding rings, which he had bought from the best jeweller of Montreal, and which had already been engraved with their names.

Then the marriage contract was read, in the loud, intelligible voice of a good lawyer, and much emotion was expressed when Mr. Nick announced that M. de Vaudreuil, out of friendship to his tenant, Thomas Harcher, had added a sum of five hundred dollars to the bride's dowry.

Five hundred dollars! when, only half a century before, a bride with a dowry of fifty francs had been considered a splendid match!

'And now, my friends,' Mr. Nick announced, 'we shall proceed to the signing of the contract. The young couple first, then the father and mother, then Monsieur and Mademoiselle de Vaudreuil, then . . .'

'We'll all sign!' came a shout that almost deafened the lawyer.

And then old and young, friends and relatives, came one after the other to add their signatures to the contract which was to assure the future of the two young people.

That took some time! Even the passers-by had now entered the farm, attracted by the joyous uproar within, and they too put their signatures to the deed, so that pages and pages would have to be added if this were to continue. And why should not the whole village, and even the whole county, crowd in, when Thomas Harcher was offering his visitors a choice of the most varied drinks, as well as the whisky that flows as naturally down the Canadian throats as the St. Lawrence towards the Atlantic?

Mr. Nick wondered if the ceremony were ever to end. The worthy man was beaming with joy; he was inexhaustible; he had a cheery word for everyone, while Lionel, passing the pen from hand to hand, realised that he would soon need a new one, as it was being worn out by the interminable column of signatures that grew ever longer and longer.

' Is that all? ' Mr. Nick asked an hour later.

' Not yet! ' Pierre Harcher had gone to the door to see if anyone were on the road.

' Who's coming now? ' enquired Mr. Nick.

' A tribe of Hurons! '

' Let them come in! Let them come in! ' the notary exclaimed. ' Their signatures will do no dishonour to the contracting parties. What a contract it is, my friends! I've drawn up hundreds in the course of my life, but never have I seen the names of so many good people at the foot of the last page! '

When the Indians appeared they were greeted with loud shouts of welcome. They did not wait for an invitation, but swarmed in, fifty in number—men and women alike. And among them Thomas Harcher recognised the Huron who had appeared the day before to ask if Mr. Nick were coming to Chipogan Farm.

Why had the Mahogannis Tribe come from their village at Walhatta? Why had they come in ceremonial attire to visit the Montreal lawyer?

There must certainly be some important reason for this.

The Hurons were all—as they are only on the most ceremonial occasions—in full war-paint. Their heads were surmounted with feathers, their long thick hair fell on to their shoulders, from which hung a multi-coloured cloak; their bodies were clad in deerskin; their feet were shod with elk-leather moccasins; they were armed with

the long rifles which for many years had replaced the
bows and arrows of their ancestors. But the traditional
axe, the war-tomahawk, hung from their belts.

Moreover—and this showed even more clearly the
seriousness of the occasion—a coat of fresh paint
bedecked their faces. Azure blue, soot and vermilion,
brought into astonishing relief their aquiline noses, their
large nostrils, their huge mouths with a double row of
regularly-curved teeth, their high, square cheek-bones,
and their small, keen eyes, whose black pupils glowed
like embers.

The deputation was accompanied by a few of the
Walhatta women — doubtless the youngest and best-
looking of the tribe. These squaws wore a bodice of
embroidered stuff, the sleeves leaving the forearm bare, a
petticoat of glaring colours, ' mitasses ' of cariboo leather,
ornamented with hedgehog quills and laced on their legs,
while soft mocassins decorated with glass beads imprisoned their feet, whose smallness a Frenchwoman might
well have envied.

The Indians had, if possible, redoubled their habitual
gravity. With much ceremony they advanced to the
threshold of the large room where stood Monsieur and
Mademoiselle de Vaudreuil, the lawyer, and Thomas
and Catherine Harcher, the rest of the party being out in
the courtyard.

Then he who seemed to be the chief, a tall Huron about
fifty years old, holding in his hand a cloak of native work,
addressed the farmer solemnly:

' Is Nicholas Sagamore at the farm of Chipogan? '

' He is here! ' replied Thomas Harcher.

' And I will add that I am he,' the lawyer was amazed
that he could be the object of their visit.

F

The Huron turned towards him, raised his head proudly, and in tones even more impressive he announced:

' The chief of our tribe has been called by the great Wacondah, the Mitsimanitou of our fathers. Five moons have passed since he went to the Happy Hunting-grounds. His heir is now Nicholas, the last of the Sagamores. To him henceforth belongs the right of burying the tomahawk of peace, or disinterring the tomahawk of war.'

A deep amazed silence greeted this unexpected declaration. It was well known in the country that Mr. Nick was of Huron origin, and that he was descended from the great chief of the Mahogannis Tribe; but no one had ever imagined—and he least of all—that the order of heredity would call him to the leadership of an Indian Tribe.

And then, amid a silence that none dare break, the Indian asked:

' And when will my brother take his seat at the fire of the Great Council of his tribe, clad in the traditional robe of his ancestors? '

The spokesman of the deputation could not imagine for a moment that the lawyer would refuse, and he solemnly gave him the robe.

And as Mr. Nick, completely dumbfounded, hesitated what to reply, there was a shout—in which fifty others joined—of:

' Honour! Honour to Nicholas Sagamore! '

It was Lionel who had raised the enthusiastic shout. That he was proud of the good fortune that had come to his master, and considered that the distinction would be reflected upon the clerks in his office, and more especially upon himself; that he rejoiced at the idea of henceforth marching by the side of the great chief of the Mahogan-nis—that goes without saying.

De Vaudreuil and his daughter could not help smiling at the astonished expression of Mr. Nick. Poor man! While the farmer and his wife, his children and his friends, offered him their sincere congratulations, he did not know what to reply.

Then the Indian again asked him the question from which there was no escape.

' Will Nicholas Sagamore follow his brothers to the wigwams of Walhatta? '

Mr. Nick was still gaping. Certainly he would never agree to forsake his profession to rule over a Huron tribe. But, on the other hand, he did not like to hurt by a refusal the Indians of his own race who were summoning him by the right of succession to such an honour.

' Mahogannis,' he said at last, ' I did not expect this. I am indeed unworthy of it. You understand—my friends —I am here only as a lawyer! '

He stammered; he was at a loss for words; he could not reply further.

Thomas Harcher came to his assistance.

' Hurons! Mr. Nick is Mr. Nick at least till this marriage ceremony is completed. After that, if it pleases him, he will leave the farm of Chipogan and will be free to return with his brothers to Walhatta! '

' Yes! After the wedding! ' shouted the others; they all wanted to keep the lawyer with them.

The Huron shook his head, but after consulting the deputation, he declared :

' My brother cannot hesitate. The blood of the Mahogannis runs in his veins and imposes upon him rights and duties which he will not wish to refuse . . .'

' Rights! rights! Agreed! ' murmured Mr. Nick, ' but duties . . .'

' Does he accept? ' asked the Indians.

' Does he accept! ' Lionel repeated. ' I'm sure of it! And in witness of his agreement he should at once be clad in the royal mantle of the Sagamores! '

' The idiot! ' Mr. Nick muttered between his teeth. ' Why can't he keep his mouth shut.'

And the peace-loving lawyer longed to calm the stormy enthusiasm of his clerk by boxing his ears.

M. de Vaudreuil realised that Mr. Nick was only trying to gain time. Addressing the Indians, he said that assuredly the descendant of the Sagamores did not think of withdrawing from the duties that his descent imposed upon him. But a few days, a few weeks perhaps, were necessary for him to put matters in order at Montreal. It was necessary, therefore, to give him time to clear things up.

' That is only wise,' the Indian agreed. ' And as my brother accepts, let him receive as the pledge of his acceptance the tomahawk of the great chief called by the Wacondah to the Happy-Hunting-grounds, and let him wear it in his belt! '

Mr. Nick took the favourite weapon of the Indian tribes, and, much perplexed at not having a belt, he simply rested it upon his shoulder.

The deputation then gave the traditional ' How! ' of their race, an exclamation of approval common to all the Indian languages.

Although his master seemed greatly embarrassed at a position which might make him a laughing-stock in the brotherhood of Canadian lawyers, Lionel could hardly restrain himself for joy. With his poetic gifts he saw that he was already called upon to celebrate the mighty deeds of the Mahogannis, and to chant in lyric verse the war cry of the Sagamores—though how he was to find a rhyme for tomahawk he did not quite see.

The Hurons were about to retire, regretting that Mr. Nick's duties prevented him from accompanying them, when Catherine had an idea.

'Mahogannis,' she announced, 'it is a marriage feast that brings us together today at Chipogan Farm. Will you stay in your new chief's company? We offer you hospitality, and tomorrow you shall take your places at the feast, where Nicholas Sagamore will occupy the seat of honour.'

This evoked thunders of applause, and they rose even louder and longer when the Mahogannis accepted an invitation made so whole-heartedly.

All that Thomas Harcher had to do was to lay the wedding-table for fifty more—and this did not embarrass him in the least, for the room was large enough even for this addition to the party.

Mr. Nick had to resign himself to his fate—for he could not do otherwise—and he received the accolade of the warriors of his tribe, whom he would willingly have sent to the devil.

And as the young people danced Canadian jigs and Scottish reels, the second day of the festivities at Chipogan came to an end.

CHAPTER XII

THE DINNER

THE GREAT day had arrived—the last of the successive ceremonies of baptism, communion, and marriage, in which the good folks of Chipogan had taken such delight. The marriage of Rose Harcher and Bernard Miquelon had been celebrated in the morning before the State official, and would now take place at the church. Then, in the afternoon, the wedding feast would bring together the guests, whose numbers had received such a large addition. It was certainly time to finish, or all Laprairie County, possibly all Montreal, would have gathered at Thomas Harcher's hospitable table.

On the morrow the party would break up. The De Vaudreuils would return to the Villa Montcalm. Jean would leave the farm, and would not reappear until the day when he would lead the Reformist party. His comrades of the *Champlain* would carry on as hunters and trappers, until the time came to rejoin their adopted brother, while the family generally would continue the routine work of the farm. The Hurons would go back to Walhatta, where they meant to give Nicholas Sagamore a triumphant reception when he came for the first time to smoke the calumet by his ancestral hearth.

But Mr. Nick had been little pleased with the homage he had received. He had no intention of giving up his business for the chieftainship of any tribe, and he had been discussing this with Monsieur de Vaudreuil and Thomas Harcher, showing a perplexity so great that they had some difficulty in keeping from laughing at him.

' You're only making a joke of it,' he complained. ' It's easy to see that you haven't any throne ready to open beneath your feet.'

' My dear Nick,' M. de Vaudreuil consoled him. ' There's no need to take it so seriously.'

' And how else can I take it? '

' The braves won't insist on it when they see you're in no hurry to appear at the Mahogannis' wigwam.'

' You don't know them! ' exclaimed Mr. Nick. ' They'll never leave me alone. They'll follow me to Montreal! They'll make demonstrations I won't be able to escape! They'll besiege my door! And what will old Dolly say? You'll see how it will end—by my sallying forth with moccasins on my feet and feathers on my head! '

And Nick, who was always ready for a laugh, ended by sharing in his friend's hilarity.

But it was with his clerk that he had the chief crow to pick. Lionel—out of sheer malice—was already treating him as if he had accepted the legacy of the defunct Huron. He no longer called him Mr. Nick. He spoke to him only in the third person, and only in the emphatic language of the Indians. And as it was appropriate to every warrior of the prairies, he had given him a choice of surnames, such as Elkhorn or the Subtle Lizard, corresponding to those of Hawkeye or the Longue Carabine.

About eleven the procession was formed up in the courtyard. It was splendidly arranged, and would certainly have inspired a young poet, had not Lionel's muse been occupied with higher themes.

At its head were Bernard Miquelon and Rose Harcher, the one holding the other's little finger, and both beaming with happiness. Then came the de Vaudreuils, with Jean at their side; then the fathers and mothers and sisters and brothers of the happy pair; then Mr. Nick and his clerk, escorted by the whole of the Huron deputation, an honour with which the lawyer would gladly have dispensed. But to Lionel's extreme regret, his master lacked the native costume, the tattooing of his body and the colouring of his face, to worthily represent the line of the Sagamores.

The ceremony was performed with all the pomp appropriate to the Harcher family's status. There was a great ringing of bells, an impressive accompaniment of hymns and prayers, and much firing of guns. And in this noisy concert of musketry the Hurons took part with a skill and precision that would have won the approval of Natty Bumppo, the famous friend of the Mohicans.

Then the procession ceremoniously returned to the farm, but now Rose Miquelon was holding her husband's arm, nothing whatever having occurred to mar the proceedings.

Then the party separated, Mr. Nick being in no way loath to leave his Mahogannis, and breathe more at his ease in the society of his Canadian friends. And more piteously than ever he kept telling M. de Vaudreuil, ' I really don't know how I'm to get rid of these savages! '

Meanwhile if any man was busy, hustled about, and stormed at from noon to three—the hour at which in accordance with ancient custom the wedding feast was to begin—that man was Thomas Harcher. True, Catherine and her sons and daughters did all they could to help him; but the preparation of a feast of this importance left him not a minute's respite.

It was not only the number of empty stomachs he had to satisfy but the diversity of tastes. And the bill of fare comprised all the ordinary and extraordinary dishes known to Canadian cookery.

On the immense table—at which one hundred and fifty guests were to sit—were set out as many spoons and forks wrapped in a white napkin and flanked by a metal cup. There were no knives, for each guest had to use his or her own. There was no bread, only the maple-sugared cake being admissible at a wedding feast. The cold meats were on the table, the hot were served in due order.

There were earthen pots of hot soup, from which perfumed vapours escaped; there were fried fish and boiled fish from the fresh waters of the St. Lawrence and the lakes, trout, salmon, eels, pike, white fish, shad, touradis and maskinongis; there were ducks, pigeons, quails, woodcock, snipe, and fricasseed squirrels; there were turkeys, geese, bustards, fattened on the farm, some roasted to a sparkling golden brown, some drowned in a sea of spice; there were hot oyster patties, forcemeat pies, huge onions, legs of mutton, chines of roast boar, maize puddings, fawn cutlets, and deer steaks; then those wonderful haunches of venison, which make Canada the envy of the epicures the world over, the bison hump so much esteemed by the hunters of the prairies, cooked in its natural fur and garnished with fragrant leaves! Add to all these, the sauce boats in which floated relishes of a score of kinds, mountains of vegetables, brought to perfection in the last days of the Indian summer; pastry of all kinds, particularly those cracknels or fritters, for the making of which Catherine Harcher's daughters enjoyed an unequalled reputation; a variety of fruit from the orchard; and a hundred flagons of different types, full of cider, beer, wine, and gin kept for the toasts at dessert.

The large room had been most artistically decorated in honour of Bernard and Rose Miquelon. Garlands of leaves ornamented the walls, appropriate shrubs stood in the corners, hundreds of nosegays of sweet-smelling flowers decorated the window bay. Moreover, guns, pistols, carbines—all the weapons of a whole family of sportsmen—were arranged in glittering trophies.

The newly-married couple were seated at the middle of the table, which was horseshoe-shaped, like the Falls of Niagara, over which, a hundred and fifty leagues to the southwest, roared their deafening cataracts. And they were indeed cataracts which were to be engulfed in the abysses of these French-Canadian stomachs!

On each side of the newly-married pair were the De Vaudreuils. Jean and his comrades from the *Champlain* were opposite, between Thomas and Catherine Harcher. Mr. Nick was enthroned with the foremost warriors of his tribe, anxious to see, no doubt, how their new chief behaved. And certainly Nicholas Sagamore promised to display an appetite worthy of his lineage. Contrary to tradition, and for this special occasion, the children were admitted to the large table among their relatives and friends, and around them moved a regiment of negroes, specially engaged for this purpose.

By five the first assault had been delivered. At six there was a truce, not to carry away the dead, but to give the living time to recover their breath. Then it was that the toasts and speeches began.

Then followed cheerful wedding songs, according to ancient custom, for whenever they met for dinner or supper, the women and the men alternately sang the old songs of France.

Then Lionel recited a flattering epithalamium composed expressly for the occasion.

' Bravo, Lionel, bravo! ' shouted Mr. Nick, who had drowned in the bowl the cares of his future sovereignty.

The dear old fellow was very proud of his young poet's success, and he proposed the health of the gallant laureate of the Lyre Amicale!

The glasses were accordingly filled to the brim, and raised towards Lionel, who was so happy and confused that he could think of no better reply than the toast:

' To Nicholas Sagamore! To the last branch of that noble tree on which the Great Spirit has hung the destinies of the Huron nation! '

There were thunders of applause. The Mahogannis stood up round the table and brandished their tomahawks as if they were about to hurl themselves against one of their ancestral enemies. Mr. Nick, with his calm face, seemed much too pacific for such bellicose warriors, and felt that this blockhead of a Lionel would have done much better to have kept silence.

When the excitement had calmed down, the second course was attacked with renewed vigour.

Amid all the din, Jean, Clary and her father had every facility for conversing in low tones. In the evening they were to separate. The De Vaudreuils were not to leave till the morning, but Jean had decided to go that night so as to seek a safer refuge than Chipogan Farm.

' But,' said M. de Vaudreuil, ' would the police think of looking for Jean-Sans-Nom among Thomas Harcher's family? '

' Who knows if the detectives aren't already on my

track?' Jean spoke as if he had some presentiment of evil, 'and if that should happen, when the farmer and his sons learn who I am . . .'

'They'll defend you,' Clary broke in. 'They'd die for you.'

'I know that,' Jean replied, 'and then in return for the hospitality they have given me I should leave behind me nothing but ruin and misfortune! Thomas Harcher and his children would be turned out of their home for having defended me! And that's why I'm so anxious to get away from the farm.'

'Why don't you return secretly to the Villa Montcalm?' asked M. de Vaudreuil. 'The risks which you want to spare Thomas Harcher from are the very ones to which it's my duty to expose myself, and I am quite ready to do so! In my house the secret of your presence would be well kept.'

'Mademoiselle de Vaudreuil has already suggested this to me in your name, but I felt I had to decline it.'

'But,' M. de Vaudreuil pointed out, 'it would be convenient for the last steps you have to take. You could keep in daily touch with the members of the committee. When the rising breaks out, Farran, Clerc, Hodge and I are ready to follow you. Isn't it quite likely that the first outbreak will take place near Montreal?'

'That is so,' said Jean, 'or rather somewhere in the neighbourhood, according to the positions which the royal troops take up.'

'Well, then,' said Clary, 'why don't you accept father's offer? Are you intending to make another tour of the neighbourhood? Haven't you finished your propaganda?'

'It's finished,' Jean replied, 'and now I've only to give the signal.'

'Then what are you waiting for?' asked M. de Vaudreuil.

'I am waiting for something to exasperate the Reformists completely,' Jean explained, 'and that will happen soon. In a few days the opposition Deputies are going to refuse the Governor the right he claims to dispose of the public revenues without the authority of the Chamber. Besides, I know from a sure source that the English Parliament means to pass a law authorising Lord Gosford to suspend the seventeen ninety-one constitution. The result will be that the French-Canadians will be left without any guarantee of a share in the representative system granted to the colony, which, even as things are, leaves them so little freedom of action! Our friends, and with them the liberal deputies, will resist this usurpation of power. Lord Gosford, to put a check on the Reformist demands, will probably dissolve or prorogue the Chamber. The day he does so the country will rise, and all we shall have to do will be to direct the revolution.'

'There's no doubt,' M. de Vaudreuil agreed, 'that such a provocation on the part of the loyalists will lead to a general revolt. Then the English Parliament will hardly dare to go so far. If this attempt against the rights of the French-Canadians does take place, are you sure it will be so soon?'

'In a few days,' Jean asserted. 'Sebastien Gramont told me so.'

'And till then,' asked Clary, 'how are you going to escape?'

'I must throw the detectives off the track.'

'Have you any hiding-place in mind?'

'I have.'

'Where you will be safe?'

' Safer than anywhere else.'

' Far away? '

' At St. Charles, in Verchères County.'

' Very well,' said M. de Vaudreuil. ' Nobody can be a better judge of this matter than yourself. If you think you can keep your hiding-place secret, we won't press our offer. But don't forget that at any hour of the day or night the Villa Montcalm will be open to you.'

' I know it, Monsieur de Vaudreuil, and I thank you.'

Amid the incessant exclamations of the guests, in the increasing tumult of the room, it may well be believed that no one had heard this conversation, which had been carried on in low tones. Occasionally it was interrupted by some noisy toast or striking repartee, or by a rousing chorus. And it seemed about to finish when Clary asked a question that evoked a very surprising reply.

What was it prompted her to ask this question? Was it some suspicion or simply a regret that Jean thought it his duty to retain a certain reserve towards her?

' So somewhere there's a house where you can hide that's more hospitable than ours? '

' More hospitable? No! But quite as hospitable,' Jean replied, not without emotion.

' And which is it? '

' My mother's.'

Jean uttered the words in such a tone of filial affection that Clary was deeply moved. It was the first time that he, whose past had been so mysterious, had ever alluded to his family. So he was not alone in the world as his friends had thought. He had a mother who was living in secret in the village of St. Charles where, no doubt, he sometimes went to see her. The house was open to him when he required quiet and rest. And it was there he was going to wait for the battle to open.

Clary made no answer. Her thoughts were drawn towards this distant house. How happy she would be to know this mother! She must be a heroic woman, a patriot whom she would love, a patriot whom she loved already! Assuredly she would see her some day. Was not her life indissolubly bound up with that of Jean-Sans-Nom, and who was it could break the bond? Yes, at the moment when she was about to part from him, perhaps for ever, she felt the power of the attraction that drew them together.

The feast was near its close, and the gaiety of the guests, stimulated by the many toasts, was showing itself in a variety of ways. Compliments to the happy couple were flowing in from all sides. It was a very good-humoured uproar, amid which could be heard every now and then:

'Honour and happiness to the young people!'

'Long live Bernard and Rose Miquelon!'

And there was health-drinking to Monsieur de Vaudreuil and his daughter, and to Catherine and Thomas Harcher.

Mr. Nick had done justice to the repast. If he had not been able to retain the austere dignity of a Mahoganni it was because that was contrary to his open, friendly nature. But it must be added that even the representatives of his tribe had somewhat departed from their ancestral gravity under the influence of the good cheer and good wine.

They had filled their glasses in the French style to salute the Harcher family, whose guests they were, when Lionel, who could not keep still, was going round the table with a compliment addressed to everyone whom he passed. It suddenly came into his head to address Mr. Nick:

' Nicholas Sagamore, won't you say a few words in the name of the tribe of Mahogannis? '

In the happy temper in which Mr. Nick was now, he did not receive the suggestion unkindly.

' Do you think so, Lionel? ' he asked.

' If you think, great chief, that the time is come for you to wish happiness to the bride and the bridegroom.'

' If you think this is the time I will do so! ' And the worthy man arose and demanded silence by a gesture full of Huron dignity.

There was an immediate lull.

' Young people,' he began, ' an old friend of your family cannot leave you without expressing his acknowledgments for . . .'

Suddenly Mr. Nick stopped. The sentence broke off upon his lips. His eyes were directed towards the door.

A man was standing on the threshold, a man whose arrival nobody had noticed.

Mr. Nick had just recognised him, and he exclaimed in surprise mingled with alarm:

' Mr. Rip! '

CHAPTER XIII

MUSKETRY AT DESSERT

THE HEAD of the house of Rip and Co. was accompanied—but not by his own men.

Behind him were a dozen of the official police, as well as forty of the loyalist volunteers, who were blocking the main entrance into the courtyard. The whole house seemed to be surrounded.

Was it a mere domiciliary visit or was the head of the Harcher family threatened with arrest? Certainly it must be a grave matter to induce the Chief of Police to send so strong a detachment to Chipogan Farm.

On hearing Rip's name, M. de Vaudreuil and his daughter were terror-stricken. They knew that Jean-Sans-Nom was in this very room. They knew that to Rip the duty of tracing him had been specially entrusted. And what could they think but that he had discovered his victim's hiding-place and was about to arrest him? If Jean fell into the hands of the police he was lost.

By a supreme effort of the will, Jean had not as much as started when he heard the name; even his colour had hardly changed. No movement, not even an involuntary one, had betrayed him; and yet he had just recognised Rip, whom he had met the day the buggy brought Nick and Lionel from Montreal. Rip, who had been hunting him for two months! Rip, the *provocateur*, who had brought infamy upon his family when he had led his father, Simon Morgaz, into treachery!

And yet he was cool and collected, and showed no sign of the hatred which raged within him, even though M. de Vaudreuil and his daughter were trembling beside him.

But if Jean knew Rip, Rip did not know him. The man did not realise that the traveller whom he had met for a moment on the road from Montreal was the very man on whose head a price had been set. All that he knew was that Jean-Sans-Nom should be at Chipogan Farm. And here he was once more upon his track!

A few days earlier Jean had been noticed five or six leagues from Saint-Charles, after he had left Maison-Close, and had been reported as a suspicious stranger while he was leaving Verchères County. Realising that the alarm had been given, he had fled into the interior of the county, and, not without many narrow escapes from falling into the hands of the police, he had reached Thomas Harcher's farm.

But Rip's men had not lost sight of him, as he had thought, and soon they were almost certain that he had taken refuge at Chipogan. Rip was at once notified. Knowing not only that the farm belonged to M. de Vaudreuil, but that the latter was there at that very time, Rip never doubted that the stranger was Jean-Sans-Nom; and after giving orders to some of his men to mix with the guests at Harchers', he had reported to the Chief of Police, who had put at his disposal a squad of police and a detachment of volunteers from Montreal. And it was in such circumstances that Rip had just appeared in the doorway, confident that Jean-Sans-Nom was among the guests of the Chipogan farmer.

It was five in the afternoon. The lamps had not yet

been lit, and it was still light in the room. Rip had at once
glanced round the company, but he paid Jean-Sans-Nom
no more attention than anyone else.

Thomas Harcher, seeing his courtyard invaded by a
body of men, rose and confronted Rip:

' Who are you? '

' I have my orders from the Chief of Police.'

' What are you doing here? '

' You shall soon know. Are you not Thomas Harcher
of Chipogan, and one of M. de Vaudreuil's tenants? '

' Yes, and I demand to know by what right you enter
my house.'

' In accordance with the duty that has been entrusted
to me, I am here to make an arrest.'

' An arrest! ' exclaimed the farmer . . . ' An arrest in
my house! And who is it you are going to arrest? '

' A man for whose apprehension a reward has been
offered by the Governor, and who is here! '

' His name? '

'He calls himself,' Rip declared loudly, 'or rather he
is known as, Jean-Sans-Nom! '

The reply was followed by a murmur. What! So it was
Jean-Sans-Nom whom Rip had come to arrest, and whom
he declared to be at Chipogan Farm!

The attitude of the farmer, of his wife and his children,
and of all present, was so obviously one of profound
astonishment, that Rip thought his men must be on a
false scent. Yet he reiterated his demand, and this time
even more decidedly.

' Thomas Harcher,' he said, ' the man I am looking for
is here, and I order you to deliver him up.'

At these words Thomas Harcher looked at his wife,
and Catherine, gripping his arm, said:

'Tell him what he ought to know.'

'Yes, Thomas,' added Mr. Nick, 'tell him. I don't think that should be difficult.'

'Quite easy, in fact.' Turning towards Rip the farmer declared, 'Jean-Sans-Nom is not at Chipogan Farm.'

'And I say he is, Thomas Harcher!' was Rip's quiet reply.

'No, I tell you, he isn't! He's never been here! I don't know him! But I say that if he had come to ask me for shelter I would have given it him, and if he were in this house I should not give him up!'

There could be no mistake about the significant demonstrations with which the farmer's declaration was received. Thomas Harcher had expressed the feelings of everybody present. If Jean-Sans-Nom had taken refuge at the farm there was not one who could be base enough to betray him.

Jean, impassive all the time, was quietly listening. Neither M. de Vaudreuil nor Clary dared even look at him for fear of drawing Rip's attention to him.

'Thomas Harcher,' continued Rip, 'you are doubtless aware that by a proclamation, dated the 3rd of September, eighteen thirty-seven, a reward of six thousand dollars is offered to whoever will arrest this Jean-Sans-Nom or who gives information leading to his arrest.'

'I know it,' said the farmer, 'and everybody in Canada knows it. But there has not yet been found a Canadian base enough to commit so odious a betrayal, and there never will be.'

'Well spoken, Thomas!' exclaimed Catherine, and her children and friends encouraged her.

Rip was unmoved.

'Thomas Harcher,' he continued, 'if you already know

that proclamation, perhaps you do not know about the new announcement which the Governor-General made yesterday, under date of the sixth of October! '

' I do not know about it,' the farmer replied, 'and if it's like the other, and simply encourages treachery, you needn't tell me about it.'

' You shall hear it all the same,' Rip produced a document and began to read:

' ' It is required of all inhabitants of the Canadian towns and country that they should refuse any help and protection to Jean-Sans-Nom, on pain of death to anyone who shelters him.

' For the Governor-General,
' Gilbert Argall,
Minister of Police.'

And so the Government had dared go to this length! After offering a reward for Jean-Sans-Nom, they had now threatened with the death penalty anyone who gave him shelter!

This unjustifiable act evoked the most violent protests on the part of all present. Thomas Harcher, his sons and his guests had risen from their seats and were about to fall upon Rip and to drive him from the farm with all his police and volunteers with him, when Mr. Nick interposed.

He looked serious. Like the rest of those present, he felt a very natural horror at the new announcement which Rip had just read.

' Monsieur Rip,' he declared, ' he whom you seek is not at Chipogan Farm. Thomas Harcher has told you so, and I reiterate it. So you have nothing to do here, and you would have done better to have kept that disgraceful document in your pocket. Believe me. Monsieur Rip, you would be well advised not to force your presence on us any longer.'

' Well said, Nicholas Sagamore! ' exclaimed Lionel.

' Yes! Get out—at once! ' said the farmer, whose voice trembled with anger. ' Jean-Sans-Nom isn't here! But if he comes, in spite of the Governor's threats, I shall welcome him! Now get out of the house! Get out, I say! '

' Yes! yes! Get out of it! ' shouted Lionel, whose exasperation Mr. Nick was vainly trying to calm.

' Take care, Thomas Harcher! ' replied Rip, ' you can't withstand the law, nor the force I have to support me. Police and volunteers together, I have fifty men with me. Your house is surrounded.'

' Get out! Clear out! '

Then shouts arose, and threats were hurled against Rip.

' I won't go until I've made sure of the identity of all present! ' Rip declared.

And as he gestured to the police in the courtyard they approached the door ready to enter the room.

Through the windows M. de Vaudreuil and his daughter could see the volunteers posted all round the house.

In view of an imminent collision, the children and women, with the exception of Clary and Catherine, were hustled into the other rooms. Pierre Harcher and his brothers and friends were taking down the weapons hanging on the walls. But inferior as they were in numbers, how could they prevent Rip from doing his duty?

M. de Vaudreuil went from window to window to see if Jean could make his escape in the rear of the farm by crossing the garden. But in this direction, as in the others, flight was impracticable.

Amid the tumult Jean stood motionless by the side of Clary, who would not leave him.

Mr. Nick then tried a last effort at conciliation, as the police were about to enter the room.

' Mr. Rip! Mr. Rip! ' he exclaimed,: ' you're going to cause bloodshed, and quite uselessly, I assure you! I repeat, and I give you my word, Jean-Sans-Nom is not at the farm.'

' And if he were,' Thomas Harcher declared, ' I repeat, I would fight for him to the death! '

' Good! Good! ' exclaimed Catherine, full of enthusiasm at her husband's attitude.

' Don't you interfere in this matter, Mr. Nick!' Rip snorted. ' It doesn't concern you, and you may have to repent it later! I mean to do my duty whatever happens! And now, make room there! Make room! '

A dozen police entered the room, and Thomas Harcher and his friends rushed at them to turn them out and shut the door.

But Mr. Nick made one last effort:

' Jean-Sans-Nom is not here. Mr. Rip, I assure you he is not here! '

' He is here! ' said a loud voice that made itself heard above the din.

There was silence for a moment.

Jean, motionless and with his arms crossed, looked Rip straight in the face and said:

' I am Jean-Sans-Nom! '

M. de Vaudreuil had seized the young man's arm, while Thomas Harcher and the others were exclaiming:

' He! He—Jean-Sans-Nom? '

Jean showed with gesture that he wanted to speak. There was another momentary silence.

' I am the man whom you seek,' he told Rip; ' I am Jean-Sans-Nom.'

And then, turning to the farmer and his sons, he continued:

' Forgive me, Thomas Harcher, forgive me, my brave companions, if I have hidden from you who I am, and let me thank you for the hospitality which for five years I have received at Chipogan farm. But the hospitality which I accepted so long as it caused you no danger, I can accept no longer now that it means death to all who give me shelter! Yes, thanks on the part of him who was here only as your adopted son, but who for his country is Jean-Sans-Nom! '

An indescribable movement of enthusiam received this declaration.

' *Vive* Jean - Sans - Nom! *Vive* Jean - Sans - Nom! ' resounded on all sides.

And when the shouts had died away, Thomas Harcher said:

' And now, as I said we'd fight for Jean-Sans-Nom, we'll fight for him to the death.'

In vain Jean would have interposed to stop so unequal a strife. No one was listening. Pierre and the older men were throwing themselves on the police who were blocking the doorway and thrusting them out. The door was at once shut and barricaded with the heavy furniture. To get into the room, or even into the house, the only way was by the windows, which were a dozen feet from the ground.

An attack would have to be made, and that in the darkness, for the night had begun to fall. Rip, who was not a man to give way, took steps to execute his warrant and to launch the volunteers against the house.

Pierre Harcher, with his brothers and friends, took up positions at the windows ready to fire.

'We will defend you, in spite of yourself, if we have to' they assured Jean, who was now powerless to stop them.

At the last moment the farmer had prevailed on Clary de Vaudreuil and Catherine to rejoin the other women in one of the side rooms, where they would be out of harm's way. Only the men were left in the room—thirty in all.

For the Mahogannis could not be reckoned among the defenders of the farm. The Indians were indifferent to all that had passed, and had maintained their habitual reserve. The matter did not concern them any more than it did Mr. Nick and his clerk, who need not take sides either for or against authority: and the lawyer meant to remain absolutely neutral. Determined neither to give nor to receive a blow, he never stopped his appeals to Lionel, who was breathing out fire and flame. Bah! the young clerk scarcely heard him, so excited was he at the chance of fighting for Jean-Sans-Nom, who was not only the popular hero, but also the sympathetic auditor who had given so favourable a hearing to his attempts at poetry.

'For the last time,' said Mr. Nick, 'I forbid you to get mixed up in this matter!'

'And for the last time,' Lionel retorted, 'I am amazed that a descendant of the Sagamores should refuse to follow me on the war-path!'

'I will follow no other path but that of peace, you stupid boy, and you'll do me the favour of leaving this room, where you can only get hurt!'

'Never!' exclaimed the bellicose poet.

And leaping at one of the Mahogannis he seized the tomahawk that hung from the man's belt.

As soon as he saw that his companions had decided to meet force with force, Jean began to organise the resistance. During the struggle he might manage to escape, and now, whatever might happen, the farmer and his people were in open rebellion against authority, and could not be more compromised than they were already. Rip and his men had first to be driven off. Then he could see what was best to be done. If the assailants tried to break in the doors of the house, that would take time. And before reinforcements arrived from Laprairie and Montreal, police and volunteers might be driven out of the courtyard. And so Jean resolved to make a sortie and clear the approaches to the Farm.

Arrangements were made accordingly. To begin with, a score of gunshots rattled from the front windows, and Rip and his men had to retreat to the palisades. Then the door was thrown open, and Jean, followed by Monsieur de Vaudreuil, Thomas Harcher, and several of the others, rushed into the courtyard.

A few of the volunteers were already lying on the ground. Some of the defenders had also been wounded, as in the semi-darkness they hurled themselves on the besiegers. A hand-to-hand struggle followed, in which Rip bravely took his share. But his men began to lose ground; if they were to be driven out of the gate and have it shut against them, they would find it difficult to get back over the high palisading.

To drive them out, Jean and his gallant companions made every effort. If they succeeded, he might be able to get away across country, and even beyond the Canadian frontier, to wait till the time came for him to reappear at the head of the insurgents.

It need not be said, that although Lionel had gallantly joined the combatants, Mr. Nick had not left the house. Determined to maintain strict neutrality, he did no more than to wish well to Jean-Sans-Nom and all the defenders, among whom he had so many personal friends.

But notwithstanding their courage, the inhabitants of the farm could not make head against the police and volunteers, who began to get the better of them. Little by little they had to retreat towards the house for shelter. The room would then be invaded, all possibility of escape would be cut off, and Jean-Sans-Nom would have to surrender.

And the forces of the besieged were perceptibly diminishing. Already two of the elder Harchers, Michael and Jacques, and three or four of their companions had been carried into one of the adjoining rooms, where Clary de Vaudreuil, Catherine, and the other women took care of them. And the battle would be lost if some reinforcement did not come to Jean's rescue.

Suddenly there came a complete change of fortune.

Lionel had just dashed into the room, covered with blood from a flesh wound in his shoulder.

Mr. Nick caught sight of him.

'Lionel! Lionel! he exclaimed, ' you wouldn't listen to me, you obstinate boy! '

And seizing the young clerk in his arms, he tried to drag him into the room where the wounded were being cared for.

Lionel refused.

'It's nothing! It's nothing! ' he protested. ' But, Nicholas Sagamore, will you let your friends be beaten, when your warriors are only waiting for a word from you to go to the rescue? '

' No! No! ' exclaimed Mr. Nick, ' I haven't the right to give it! To take part against the constituted authorities! '

And with one supreme effort he threw himself among the combatants, anxious to stop them by his entreaties.

He met with no success. On the other hand, he was at once surrounded by the police and dragged out into the courtyard.

This was too much for the Mahoganni warriors, whose bellicose instincts could not stand such an insult. What! Their great chief to be arrested and ill-treated! A Sagamore in the hands of his enemies, the Pale-faces!

It was too much! And the war-cry resounded high above the din of battle.

' Forward! Forward! Hurons! ' shouted Lionel, who by this time was quite beside himself.

The intervention of the Indians at once changed the fortunes of the war. Tomahawk in hand, they hurled themselves at their assailants, who, already exhausted by an hour's fighting, were beginning to retreat.

Jean-Sans-Nom, Thomas Harcher, and their friends felt that a well-delivered effort would drive Rip and his men out of the yard. Once more they took the offensive. The Hurons vigorously helped them, after rescuing Mr. Nick, who was astonished to find himself encouraging them with his voice if not with his hand, which could not yet flourish the ancestral tomahawk.

And that was how a Montreal lawyer, the most pacific of men, got into danger for defending a cause which had nothing to do either with the Mahogannis or with their chief!

Police and volunteers alike were soon driven out of the gate, and as the Indians pursued them for a mile across country, Chipogan was completely cleared.

It was obviously a bad business, and would figure on the wrong side in the next profit and loss account of Messrs. Rip and Co.

Victory on this day had come not to the law but to the forces of patriotism.

APPENDIX

LIONEL'S ODE

As an example of Verne's poetic work, this deserves to be quoted in the original:

Le Feu Follet

Ce feu fantasque, insaisissable,
Qui, le soir, se dégage et luit,
Et qui, dans l'ombre de la nuit,
Ni sur la mer ni sur la sable,
Ne laisse de trace après lui!

Ce feu toujours prêt à s'éteindre,
Tantôt blanchâtre ou violet,
Pour reconnaître ce qu'il est,
Il faudrait le pouvoir atteindre . . .
Atteignez donc un feu follet!

On dit, est-ce chose certaine?
Que c'est l'hydrogène du sol.
J'aime mieux croire qu'en son vol,
Il vient d'une étoile lointaine,
De Véga, de la Lyre, ou d'Algol.

Mais n'est-ce pas plutôt l'haleine
D'un sylphe, d'un djinn, d'un lutin,
Qui brille, s'envole et s'éteint,
Lorsque se réveille la plaine
Aux rayons joyeux du matin?

Ou la lueur de la lanterne
Du long spectre qui va s'asseoir

190

Sur la chaume du vieux pressoir,
Quand la lune, blafarde et terne,
Se lève à l'horizon du soir?

Peut-être l'âme lumineuse
D'une folle qui va cherchant
La paix hors du monde méchant,
Et passe comme une glaneuse
Qui n'a rien trouvé dans son champ?

Serait-ce un effet de mirage,
Produit par le trouble de l'air,
Sur l'horizon déjà moins clair,
Ou, vers la fin de quelque orage,
Le reste d'un dernier éclair?

Est-ce la lueur d'un bolide.
D'un météore icarien,
Qui, dans sa course aérien,
Etait lumineux et solide,
Et dont il ne reste plus rien?

Ou sur les champs dont il éclaire
D'un pâle reflet le sillon,
Quelque mystérieux rayon
Tombé d'une aurore polaire,
Comme une nocturne papillon?

Serait-ce en ces heures funèbres,
Où les vivants dorment lassés,
Le pavillon aux plis froissés
Qu'ici-bas l'Ange des ténèbres
Arbore au nom des trépassés?

Ou bien, au milieu des nuits sombres,
Lorsque le moment est venu,
Est-ce le signal convenu
Que la terre, du sein des ombres,
Envoie au ciel vers l'inconnu,

Et qui, comme un feu de marée,
Aux esprits errants à travers
Les vagues espaces ouverts,
Indique la céleste entrée
Des ports de l'immense Univers?

Mais si c'est l'amour, jeune fille,
Qui l'agite à tes yeux là-bas,
Laisse le seul a ses ébats!
Prends garde a ton coeur! Ce feu brille ...
Il brille mais ne brûle pas!

Qui que tu sois, éclair, souffle, âme,
Pour mieux pénétrer tes secrets,
O feu fantasque, je voudrais
Pouvoir m'absorber dans ta flamme!
Alors partout je te suivrais.

Lorsque sur la cime des arbres,
Tu viens poser ton front ailé,
Ou, discrètement appelé,
Lorsque tu caresses les marbres
Du cimetière désolé!

Ou quand tu rôdes sur les lisses
Du navire battu de flanc
Sous les coup du typhon hurlant,
Et quand dans les agrès tu glisses
Comme une lumineux goéland!

Et l'union serait complète
Si le destin, un jour, voulait
Que je puisse, comme il me plaît,
Naître avec toi, flamme follette,
Mourir avec toi, feu follet!